Sulaiman Addonia is an Eritrean-Ethiopian-British novelist. He spent his early life in a refugee camp in Sudan, and his early teens in Jeddah, Saudi Arabia. He arrived in London as an under-age unaccompanied refugee without a word of English and went on to earn an MA in Development Studies from SOAS and a BSc in Economics from UCL.

His first novel, *The Consequences of Love* (Chatto & Windus, 2008), was shortlisted for the Commonwealth Writers' Prize and translated into more than 20 languages. His second novel, *Silence is My Mother Tongue* (Indigo Press, 2019; Graywolf, 2020), was a Finalist for the Lambda Literary Awards 2021, the Firecracker (CLMP) Awards, the inaugural African Literary Award from The Museum of the African Diaspora (MoAD) in San Francisco, and longlisted for the 2019 Orwell Prize for Fiction. Addonia's essays appear in *LitHub*, *Granta*, *Freeman's*, *The New York Times*, *De Standaard* and *Passa Porta*. He is a contributor to *Tales of Two Planets* (Penguin, 2020) and *Addis Ababa Noir* (Akashic Books, 2020).

Addonia currently lives in Brussels where he founded the Creative Writing Academy for Refugees & Asylum Seekers and the Asmara-Addis Literary Festival In Exile (AALFIE), selected in 2022 as one of the top 40 literary festivals in the world. In 2021 he was awarded Belgium's Golden Afro Artistic Award for Literature and in 2022 he was elected as a Fellow of Royal Society of Literature (RSL).

The Seers
Sulaiman Addonia

The Seers

My mother gave birth to me in Keren, but I rebirthed myself in London that spring night as I topped Bina-Balozi on a bench in Fitzroy Square. It was as if a lantern was attached to the tip of my strap-on so that as I entered him, I saw my reflection in a world inside him that was familiar and unfamiliar, beautiful and disturbing, disruptive and reaffirming. Hannah, Bina-Balozi screamed my name. I have never felt more present, surrendering as I did to my sexual power, inflating the force of my desire to breathe inside him with new ways of seeing and being seen. The O on Bina-Balozi's backside opened like a rosebud in the middle of the night. O Bina-Balozi, the fragrance of my garden. O. B. B. That night, as I tightened my grip around Bina-Balozi's waist, I whispered my story into his ears, into the London sky, a story uncensored and more truthful than my asylum application, which was gathering dust on the Home Office's shelves. And it went like this: my mother was born in Keren at sunrise on 27 March 1941, when British troops defeated the Italians who had ruled over our country for half a century. The birth took place in a house at the foot of the mountains of Keren, which had witnessed three months of battle, three months of Europeans fighting over our land, three months during which my then pregnant grandmother had bound her stomach with flower- and butterfly-print fabric as the violence of artillery fire raged nearby. To no avail. My mother came into this world and lived through it with a volcanic potency. When the child was born, the family helper searched for my grandfather, but he was out on the street celebrating another kind of birth. He waved flowers and sang his gratitude to the British soldiers who had liberated his country from fascism. A British officer turned to him and everyone around him and said: I didn't do it for you, nigger. I Didn't Do It For You. Nigger. My grandfather cried, not at his daughter's birth but at the end of one humiliation and the beginning of another. He and his country were passed from the hands of fascists into another form of European oppression. This anecdote stayed with me. It seeded my bitterness towards the British in my childhood. The Brits drew my grandfather's attention away from my mother's birth, centring themselves in his mind instead. My mother was orphaned by a man who devoted his time to everything English, from books to food, studying their way of life, as if the way to mend his shattered pride was to mirror them in style and behaviour. He used to own flat caps, but with the arrival of the British, the fedora became his favourite headgear. He bought grey suits, wearing the English weather around sunny Keren. His shirts came with cufflinks, and his waistcoats had two pockets which he filled with silk rose petals after he learnt that the rose was England's national flower – and I crooned when I unearthed the rose on Bina-Balozi's back. O Bina-Balozi. My grandfather spoke English to my mother so that it became one of her many languages. My grandmother was so enraged by my grandfather's absence from her side during labour that she gave her daughter an Italian name: Mary Malinconia. I often think about the fighting both in the mountains and at home between my grandparents, and whether the violence my mother experienced as a foetus in her mother's womb played a role in the violence she inflicted on my father, a violence that would trickle down to me and lose its teeth inside Bina-Balozi. O Bina-B, give me more of the peace inside you. This sense of a family suffering from humiliation became like a hereditary disease that had been passed down to me. When I was two, my mother was killed by the Ethiopian army, who had taken over from the Brits and colonised our country ever since. I have no memory of her. All I have told you so far was passed down to me. Like second-hand clothes, some of us march through this life with stories full of holes and gaps. But, as the Eritrean proverb taught to me by my father goes: ኩሉ ይሓልፍ ፍቅሪ ትቅጽል – *kullu yihalif, fiqri yiterif* – *everything passes, love remains*. O Bina-B. It was at Diana's in those early days of my life in London, when I wasn't allowed to go to school to learn English and my application for asylum was still under consideration, that I connected with the language of my interior. In that room at Diana's house in Kilburn, I too was shelved as I imagined my file at the Home Office to be: vertical, stacked among stories from around the world, from places this country had once occupied. I imagined our files leaning to one side, about to collapse, a waterfall of words pouring onto the floors of the Home Office, the building flooding with words. In that room at Diana's, my journey of discovery to my inner world launched my increasing flirtation with the deepest desires of my body and mind. In London, and in those early weeks, I owned nothing except time, so much that I believed the Home Office was giving me time in bucketloads to drown me in it. And on that bench in Fitzroy Square, as I pushed into Bina-B's recesses, through the rules, roles, norms, fears, doubts, I found his native language. O. B. B. Bina-Balozi turned around and threw his arms around my neck. His eyes became my mirror – seeing your reflection in the eyes of a wild lover roaming the fields of your imagination is the most sensual act. O. B. B. BB's cries of pleasure alerted a woman walking her dog. What are you doing? the woman shouted. I yelled back: What's your problem? Don't you have sex at home? That wasn't dogging. The streets of London were my home – they were where I slept, ate, washed, cried, defecated, had sex, and where I recorded the events from the point of view of my eyes... *EYES: Hannah gets up from her cardboard-box bed under her tree in Tavistock Square... a tree that has become her home following her release from her stint in prison... she yawns... the 100 dead poets of Bloomsbury sleeping rough around her scatter with the daylight except one... and she stretches in front of E.E. Cummings showering in his affirmation (i like your body / i like what it does, i like its hows)... Hannah feels hot... she twirls... takes a few steps... then... she turns around... people are dotted around the park... people eating reading crying thinking laughing looking talking... death is in town today with a bench being installed in memory of someone who has just died... but why don't memories die? Hannah asks... she remembers her family back in Eritrea waiting for her return as a fully-trained engineer... ha... ha... ha... she laughs at the thought... then cries... her breath smells of disappointment... the morning feels gloomy... London's optimism is eluding her today and Hannah thinks it's acting like a black cab that doesn't stop for black people... it's quite a job being Hannah's eyes... living under a tree... but even if she loses her sight and loses us we'll still be here because we feel with the same power and intensity as we see... we're stuck... no way out for us... ha... never mind... now more than ever it's interesting to be Hannah's eyes... (our stoic expression breaks into a brief smirk)...* O Bina-Balozi. I remember that evening when I was thirteen, the end of another day spent under foreign rule. Instead of the Brits, Eritrea was now governed by Ethiopians. My mother was dead, my country a colony, and my father was living but not alive. His mind and heart had left along with my mother. Eritrean freedom fighters armed with Kalashnikovs besieged our town.

As Ethiopian fighter planes circled above that evening, my father was in our garden. I was inside our concrete home with its green ceiling and walls covered with pictures of my mother in varying poses. My father had raised me alone, refusing to remarry, electing to live in my mother's memory. He was an encyclopaedia of her history: he taught me how she spoke, ate, drank, laughed, and how she gazed into the distance as if her thoughts gathered layers in spaces that stretched into infinity. He'd even encouraged me to mimic her routine of taking showers. My mother showered twice a day in our bathroom with its open roof at the cusp of dawn and dusk, so her skin was ready to receive light and darkness. And I can imagine now the sun rising and setting, leaving time-prints on her body that became as magical as the curves of Keren's mountains. My mother became a woman who was possessed by nature, its poetry and destructive power, its silences and roars. My father would often take me to our town's garden at night and ask me to walk through it without a torch, and I'd feel my path by tracing the scent of flowers and fruits drifting in the air. This was my father's idea of living in a war zone, one that he inherited from his family, who had lived through similar destructions: seeing through feeling beauty was necessary for those living in a country prone to cyclical violence like ours. I found affection and friendship in things other than people. I grew up attentive to the languages of nature, just like my mother. And he insisted I inherit her love for books too. And though he couldn't read or write, he collected books after her death and became known as the illiterate book collector. His mantra was ኩሉ ይሓልፍ ፍቅሪ ትቐጽል – *kullu yihalif, fiqri yiterif – everything passes, love remains*. I talked to my mother's picture on my father's wall now as the Ethiopian planes flew above our town. I told her I hated the dergue army that had killed her as much as she hated the British colonists and as much as her father had hated the Italians. This hatred became a hereditary disease so virulent that years later I'd decide to bear no children. My father came inside. He pulled out his handgun and placed it on a table next to his bed, on top of which was a large empty box that he began to fill with books. I went to the garden and was watering our pots of herbs when my father came out of the room with a pickaxe and the boxes of books. He had told me that my mother was now a star. We looked up, our eyes combing the sky. The occupier's fighter planes flew in pairs over our town, their fume trails adding layers to a clouded sky. There were no stars visible. He dug a grave-like hole. My father had collected the books of people killed in the war or those who fled to safety, leaving their belongings behind. It became his instinct to save books like some rescued abandoned pets. He didn't see the contradiction in an illiterate man stockpiling books, as pointed out to him by many in our town. He imagined himself to be like our library built by the Italians: a building with the tenderness to embrace thousands of books. He, too, would be a safe home for words, ideas, history and stories. But unlike the Italian library, by-whites-for-whites, his would be as open as the moon. I remember those evenings when our garden was packed with adults and children who had come to read my father's books whenever there was a lull in the bombardment, when women who couldn't read or write would arrive with their bun sets and make coffee and popcorn in exchange for stories, when poets would read their unfinished work to gauge their audience's reaction, when, having read some of my father's books, debates would break out among intellectuals. It was on one of those evenings, when oil lamps were scattered among our flowers, when the smell of coffee wafted through the air filled with laughter, arguments, theories, opinions, poetry, when popcorn popped under lids, that my father gave me my mother's diary and said: ኩሉ ይሓልፍ ፍቕሪ ትቕጽል – *kullu yihalif, fiqri yiterif* – *everything passes, love remains*. He couldn't have imagined that I'd be reading it for the first time in London, in an English woman's home. But in Eritrea, I read the books he'd found and now carried out of his room. Each book was preserved in me before he placed them into boxes that he buried in holes, into which he also transplanted a hibiscus, a bougainvillaea. Our garden and I became twin cemeteries for books. I was surrounded by destruction but life bubbled beneath my bones, as if my insides were the walls of Babylon. The poets of Persian civilisations whose work I feasted on entertained me throughout my insomniac childhood. I consumed so many texts on Arabic architecture that when I strolled around our neighbourhood after bombardments, I'd be rebuilding destroyed homes and schools in my head. Each building I revived in my fantasy was as radiant and colourful as those of the Andalusian era. I became a coffer for words, characters and phrases that journeyed in books from far-off lands. I empathised with Oliver Twist before I came to his country and endured poverty in London, living under my tree in Tavistock Square. I launched metaphorical avalanches of snow, which I encountered in a geography book my father saved from a burning house that belonged to an Italian teacher, onto the childhood companions I had despised. I screamed the language of Russian writers at the Ethiopian soldiers, firing revolutionary words as if my mouth were a catapult.

Literature could be a weapon too. But did it influence my fondness for asses? I don't know, but I was unfiltered, and my mind as uncensored as some of the writers I read, like the Abbasid Caliphate poet Abu Nuwas, who wrote poems about his love for men's buttocks, the mysteries hidden inside trousers. *All is love*, the poet said. All is love, I repeated. I look back and convince myself that by making me read all these books, my father assigned me to an orphanage of literature. The written words would sculpt themselves into a human-like presence that would allow me to continue to feel the love of the family I lost to war. ኩሉ ይሓልፍ ፍቅሪ ትቅጽል – *kullu yihalif, fiqri yiterif – everything passes, love remains*. After my father buried the books in our garden that last evening, he returned to his room and soon after exited dressed in a matching blue shirt and trousers, his long hair combed back. The sky roared. He looked up and searched for my mother among the stars in the planes' wake. She was nowhere to be seen. As if he sought her presence in her scent, he fetched her underwear, which he had folded into a square, and put it into the top pocket of his shirt. A man's face emerged over the top of our garden wall, beside an oil lamp. It was the news-spreader. He had news: the one streetlamp in our town, rationed by the administrator of the occupying forces, had been switched on. As our town hadn't seen the moon, stars or sun for days, the light drew out the inhabitants like a funfair on the beach. Let's hurry, Father, I said, as if longing to see and be seen before the return of darkness. I sat on his handlebars, my back curved against the breeze. As he pedalled along the dusty road, the night enveloped us, its heat penetrated my skin. I thought about my father as he guided me through the dark, empty roads. Every time he saved a book from beneath dead bodies, from burning buildings and abandoned homes, they gave him a purpose in the way a new love would. Love can come from so many places: I could see it in the way he smiled to himself each time he found a book. Some nights, he would lie awake with a book in his hand and inhale the words he couldn't understand as if that was his way of enriching the library of his emotions. When we arrived at the gate of a now-closed café located deep inside an orchard, behind the walls painted turquoise, the planes reconquered the skyline. He braked, and we disembarked. I stood beside him as his torch beams kissed the guava, orange and mango trees. Leaves changed colour with the shifting light, shadows brightened and dimmed. It was a rebirth, the way darkness opened itself to receive light. My father cried. Father, are you alright? He didn't answer. We set off again towards the streetlamp. A line of fighter planes flew low above us. The earth underneath us shook as bombs fell on the nearby mountains. My father pedalled faster along the road filled with potholes, and I hoped I'd catch his thoughts, as if they were the particles that shimmered ahead of us in his bike's headlight. But thoughts, like everything around us, were fractured. My father slowed his pedalling and flashed his torch around as if an enemy might hurl himself at us at any moment. More planes, more bombs. The horizon burst into flames, the kind of flames that claimed my mother. Our country turned into an incense burner for our flesh. Those we loved wafted with the smoke into the clouds, and clouds still bring me a sense of melancholy. ኩሉ ይሓልፍ ፍቅሪ ትቕጽል – *kullu yihalif, fiqri yiterif – everything passes, love remains.* My father swerved the bike around a car upside down next to a rubbish heap on the verge of collapsing, rabbits poking their heads out of its belly. A lorry with trees rooted on its hood welcomed us onto a row of compounds with burnt roofs. From this deserted street, my gaze climbed to the busy skyline. The moon and the stars were concealed, disquieted by violence. I imagined my mother as my father did, travelling as a star with the constellations above the clouds, above the rain, above the planes. He heaved. I turned towards him. Are you alright, Father? He didn't answer. His long hair blew in the breeze, casting a scent of abandonment around me. The sound of bleating distracted me from my thoughts. A column of goats marched towards us, their herder dozing on his donkey cart, while an oil lamp swung from his bony neck over a wounded goat tucked up on his lap. A flock of birds flew over his head. Nature was about to desert us too. Perhaps that was why my father pulled his gun and shot at the swarms in the sky, disturbing their migration and my thoughts. After we had trudged up a steep hill populated by the voices of those who had departed, and trekked past a man in black, rocking from side to side, a group of stray dogs of different breeds padded past us. A wounded man in military fatigues leant against a tree, the blood dripping from his arm feeding the fruit's roots as if enacting the metaphor chanted by the rebel fighters: We are ready to give our blood to our land. Just as my father was about to stop to aid the man, the dogs surrounded the wounded soldier and snarled at him. We continued on our way. My father gasped. I craned my head back towards him: Father, are you alright? No answer. An old woman in a traditional white zuria, its edges decorated with blue embroidery, sat alone next to an oil lamp and a coffee set on top of the rubble of a destroyed building. As she roasted coffee beans in the long-handled pan on an open furnace crammed with lit charcoals, she turned her head from left to right, talking, giggling, as if engaged in small talk with those who had died but whose souls gleamed in the flying sparks in the darkness. The air smelled of coffee. A dull sound rang out. My father pulled out his handgun and aimed at the sky, the clouds and the stars beyond them. Don't shoot, Father, I said. You might hit my mother. He put his handgun back in his pocket, and we cycled on. Clouds of smoke drawn over the town by the comings and goings of the fighter planes thickened. We had to hide from a new wave of bombardment under the veranda of an old tailor's shop, it was like waiting out tropical rainfall. A bald woman in a white dress with a guitar emerged from a house with a front garden lit by oil lamps. Nocturnal Nubian nightjars descended into her courtyard and sang as she played her instrument. My father sobbed. I traced the direction of his eyes: a sky weighed down by smoke, by the love smouldering in his gaze. Let's go, I said, pulling at his arm. I sat on the handlebars and hummed as we cycled along an empty street, and then he pedalled up a hill, standing. Once we reached a plateau, he sat back down. The night smelled of moist grass and his sweat. He hiccupped as if he'd just been crying. When we arrived at the asphalted road, we both hopped off the bike and joined the throng marching towards the streetlamp. It was as if the entire town had been reincarnated, clothed in sentimentality, as if those of us who couldn't flee the country could still escape through each other, voyaging into a world of memories stowed in each other's eyes, now visible under the streetlamp. Many embraced as if to begin a dance of goodbyes, cuddling after a long period of separation. A young man emptied a chewing-gum pack into a woman's mouth and leant forward as if to drink her warm, minted breath. Some came to read a book, students with

homework, a tailor who had lost his glasses squinted as he inserted his thread through a needle to stitch a wound. A group of youths arrived carrying a bottle of tej wine and cards. I remember how, as I gazed at the lamp, my smile became as incandescent as the bulb, and my thoughts lit up. My head burst with daydreams, as colourful as the moths flying around us. Optimism filled my mind as if the future was born at night. O Bina-B. O. B. B. I could see the light at the end of your *O*, irradiating your tunnel. The crowd around the lamp grew so enormous that a scuffle broke out. In the ensuing chaos, pickpocketing proliferated, companions lost each other, and the words between lovers in this heated ambience lost their intended meaning. Murmurs, screams, gasps, laughter, cries, moaning and mourning echoed between mouths. The return to normality ended when a bomb fell nearby and dispersed the throng.
I lost my father. The crowd shrieked. I shut my eyes and blocked my ears with my hands, and when I opened them again I found myself alone on the empty street under the glare of the light. There, in the distance, stood three soldiers. They fixed their eyes on me. I whispered my father's name. The soldiers looked at each other and smiled. They returned me bleeding to my father. My father cleaned me and put me to bed. That night, I awoke with a pain in my stomach to find my father in the garden under the lime tree next to an oil lamp, holding my mother's picture. I didn't want to interrupt him. I stood by the door and watched him. He looked up. The thick smoke that had hovered over our town for days and nights broke and, like rain-packed clouds, dispersed. The moon shone. The stars, my father said. I can see the stars. I can see her. I can see my love. He dropped to his knees and collapsed. Father. Father, are you alright?

ኩሉ ይሓልፍ ፍቅሪ ትቅጽል – *kullu yihalif, fiqri yiterif – everything passes, love remains*. O Bina-B let me dive inside you and drown in your peace. O. B.B. Bina-B danced on the floor of my lap, danced to the musicality of my story and the grief permanently lodged in my throat. Tell me more, he said, as his hips swayed on my thighs. He paused, interrupting his dance the same way someone interrupts themselves mid-sentence. People in moments of contemplation are at their sexiest, I thought. I turned him over so his back was on the bench, and as I lifted his legs in the air to probe him deeper, his pink skin flowered between his cheeks. I brought spring to his depth. O B.B, let me take you back to the day I began my journey to London, to Diana's foster home in Kilburn, and to you. After my father's death, my mother's diary and I were passed from one relative to another, beginning with an old cousin who had lost her sight but could still see inside humanity, until I arrived back at my mother's birthplace in Keren to live with my mother's helper, who had served my grandparents' family since the birth of my mother. I called her my aunt. She had a son around my age, named Alem. My aunt tied a scarf around her waist and kept on singing the same song from the day I came to live with her until the day of my departure when I turned seventeen. One day, Alem walked in on me in the open-roofed shower. From then on, the bathroom turned into an oasis where he and I discovered each other's bodies. As the war destroyed the world we were born into, we built an alternative in our bodies, and the mutual pleasure when we inserted our fingers inside the other was like a current that streamed between us, as if reciprocity were our conductor. Alem was on my mind the evening I prepared for my date with Bina-Balozi. I was a refugee, the Home Office was yet to accept me as a citizen of this country, but the *O* I constructed on the back of Bina-B was the home I had been searching for. I could be labelled mad for stating this thought, but let me say this, and of this I'm certain: all my senses are intact, despite the tragedies of my life. In fact, when it comes to accomplishing greatness, preserving my sanity has been my greatest accomplishment in an otherwise lacklustre life, and greatness is what my family back home bet on me achieving when they sent me to Europe all those years ago. Even my sex life is questionable, as I stagger from one relationship to another. In an age when clarity and definitions are of the essence, people fail to read me, but how could they when I don't know who I am. As a lover once said to me: Hannah, you've no shape, your source is ambiguous. Can anyone fuck a mystery, can anyone fall in love with a puzzle? But regardless of the heartaches I bring upon myself and others, I view the fluidity with which I live as something I don't wish to change or refine. And this 'Hannah is fucking men's assess instead of studying' is something I didn't want to shout about here. But since a fellow Eritrean refugee wrote those exact words to my family back home, I must explain it and confront those rumours head-on. I didn't let my family down, I merely elevated my desires. I remember when I stood naked in front of my wardrobe in my studio flat in Great Portland Street to prepare for my date with Bina-Balozi. I had booked a table for us at an Italian restaurant off Tottenham Court Road. My wardrobe was like a memory box. Each item reminded me of a particular moment in my history: migration, love, heartaches, a sex act, wine, fighting, homelessness, falling down and getting up again in London's streets. I curate my clothes for each particular occasion, and that allows me to recollect moments of failure or success years after an event has passed. A change of clothing alters my mood the way the London weather does. I thought about this before I picked my outfit for my dinner with Bina-Balozi. There was my brown tweed suit, a leather coat, a fichu scarf and leather shoes that I wore when I longed to be as layered as James Baldwin. I had a short-sleeved white vintage jumpsuit I purchased for my evening strolls when I learnt of London's manufacturing past: it was as if rooting myself in this city's history was the only way to fit into its present. But that night on my date with Bina-B, I wore my double-breasted trench coat and combat boots. Someone with sexual needs like mine is in a constant battle against interior and exterior forces. I whistled along to the French song 'La Vie en rose' as I tied my strap-on around my waist. The desire to make love to Bina-B was so overwhelming that it felt like the strap-on was an organ I had transplanted into my body: its roots settled into the fertile soil of my being and spread to my conscious and subconscious, the sensual and wild as well as the intellectual and spiritual sides. Lust surged through me, and the veins of my inner thighs bulged. O. B. B. I left for the restaurant where I was to meet Bina-Balozi with my long hair tied in a bun and tucked under my yellow fedora like a dark secret. On Tottenham Court Road, I passed my favourite sex shop. As I stood for a moment by the door and bathed in the warmth of the shop's rainbow-neon light, I remembered my aunt who had sent me from Eritrea to London. London became something different from what it meant to my people back home. My London was a place for those who sought a home in ambiguity, in the freedom of being here and there, one foot in the darkness and the other in the glare. It wasn't just about discovering myself but also about London discovering itself in me. That's what freedom meant to me: when the place you live in feels at home in you, with all those who make it tick. Those who let the label they were born with slip through their fingers like sand. All those who had suffered outside themselves belonged to me. I saw them because London saw itself on my neon skin. Loud. Alive. I wandered along its pathways and sleepy lanes. I breathed in the curry-scented streets with rows of council homes, the basil and oregano window boxes outside a Mediterranean restaurant, and private gated gardens bathing in Provence lavender. I strode past a man pissing near the entry of a cul-de-sac. The wind blew my fedora off and I chased after it. My mind brightened when pleasure arrived in the arms of darkness. O B.B. The *O* that stood for the rose between his black cheeks that burst open in the dark and coloured my sleepless nights, *B* for the ballet dancer on the floor of my lap. It was raining. I pushed open the door of the restaurant. A waiter welcomed me with a smile and asked if he could take my trench coat and fedora. I declined. As you wish, general, he said, winking. Well, you ruined your chances of a good tip, I said. He threw his hand in the air as he marched off. I spotted Bina-Balozi at the table I had reserved at the back. He sprang to his feet and watched me walk towards him. He took his hands out of his pockets, held them by his sides, then put them back in his pockets again. Hey, Hannah. I leant over the table and hugged him. My mind drifted back to the first time we had met at my foster carer's house in Kilburn years earlier. He hadn't changed. He was as ageless as the innocence in his eyes. Let's sit, I said, pulling out my chair. Yes, OK, he said. Nice suit, I said. Where did you buy it? Oxford Street, he said.

I hope you're not recycling it from previous dates. Yes, I mean, no. He howled. How embarrassing, he said. We laughed. There was a clatter when a diner at the table next to ours dropped a knife onto a plate. Bina-Balozi, though, kept his attention on me and said with a slight quiver: So, Hannah, how do you feel? Now or in general? Now, he said. Well, I won't lie, I'm horny, I said. Oh, OK. He cackled as he shuffled in his seat. How about in general? I shifted my fedora to the side: No difference these days, I said. Heads at tables around turned as he burst into a fit of laughter. Shush. Don't mind them, I said. Well, you can afford to be, he said. You're beautiful. I prefer the word free, I said. Right, right, he said. Well, ask me why, I said. He gulped hard, as if he'd swallowed his pride and the shock at my directness at the same time. It didn't matter. He asked what I suggested. Why, Hannah? I wanted to tell him about what happened in my room at Diana's when I first arrived in this country, and I couldn't work and study because my asylum application hadn't been approved yet, and how I learnt to live freely in my room in Kilburn that felt like a prison. But I fell silent for a moment. O BB. Bina-Balozi bowed. Can you look at me? He took a few seconds, longer than I wanted, but he raised his eyes to meet mine, full of lust, as if his libido flourished on command. He was about to lower his head, but I stopped it in time. Don't, I said. He shifted on his chair. Despite his twitchiness, a smile never left his face. BB, I said. By the way, in my dreams, I call you BB. He tittered. I searched for thoughts in his eyes and strove to quiet myself as he bit his lower lip. Gosh, you're now a university student, he said. Diana would've been proud. I snorted: What does it matter? Look at you, BB, you finished your degree and now you work at a fast-food restaurant. Bina-B leant back and folded his arms across his chest. Hannah, I'm saving for my master's, he said. It'll work out in the end. Classical music played on the restaurant's radio, and Bina-Balozi drifted into silence along with it. Actually, Hannah, BB said after a while, I brought you something. I peered into his mouth. His lips parted like curtains and I coveted the mystery inside him. O.B.B. He searched the pocket of his suit: Here, he said, to thank you for asking me out. It was a pack of vouchers to spend at the fast-food restaurant where he worked as a supervisor. This is perfect, I said. My uni grant is drying up. You're welcome, Hannah. Then he presented me with a more befitting gift: silence. I observed him as he placed his chin on the back of his hand. He was susceptible to daydreaming in company, a trait I embraced. I thought of the occasions I had abandoned sex with lovers midway through the action to continue it instead in my imagination, brimming with fantasies. But BB was different. Some of those with wounds like lava in their pores glow in my dark thoughts. O. Bina-Balozi. I let the silence roam between us. As he rubbed his forehead, his muscles tensed through his suit. How could he keep fit while working at a fast-food restaurant? My lust sauntered on his long neck, and his name, like lit firewood in my mouth, burnt me. He tilted his head to one side. O B. B. Hello again, said the waiter, interrupting my thoughts. I'll call you when we're ready, I said. He threw the menus onto the table. I was about to spring to my feet to seek him out when Bina-Balozi put his hand on mine. We can go somewhere else if you want, he said. His touch melted the frost forming between my eyebrows. I stroked the veins that popped out around his knuckles to quieten his shivers. It was the inside of him I wanted to shake. I remember we talked, exchanged stories about our pasts, I remember listening to his breathing when we fell silent, I remember thinking he was like a secluded lake shimmering in the sunlight – everything about him was an invitation to dive in. As I ogled him in silence, the piece between my thighs embedded itself deeper, its nerves attached to the wellspring of my desires, where various energies, of the sexes, the defined and undefinable, swirled, rose and resculpted into different beings. Breathless, I asked BB to pass me his hand under the table. He didn't move. BB, can I have your hand? When he gave it to me, I squeezed it and led it to my crotch. He snatched it back, jerked his head to the side and stared at the door. Bina? Silence. Bina-B, do you want to say something? I asked. BB shuffled on his chair. After a long hesitation, he said, Hannah, erm, I'm not ready for this. It's OK, I said. I'll be here when you are. He smiled. We ate, drank, talked and then ended the evening, promising to meet soonish, as I said to him. The veins between my thighs pulsated as we embraced before he fetched his umbrella from the stand by the exit. I ordered another glass of wine. The alcohol I'd learnt to drink with Diana made me drunk with memories of our late, at times silent, nights in her house in Kilburn. I was taken there by the refugee organisation. The memories of those years ticked in my chest. I drank while fighting off the melancholy, heightened by the falling rain, and left the restaurant. On Tottenham Court Road I thought about my desires and the places they were leading me to. I've been called a freak, shameless, and denounced for my decadence for having this urge to fuck a man's ass in the way they wanted to fuck me. When I arrived at Fitzroy Square after my dinner date with Bina-B, I took my shoes off so as not to disturb the dead poets who had lived in or migrated to this area, their poetic souls buried in the air of Bloomsbury, poets I discovered when I was homeless. Talking and exchanging ideas with dead poets validated my existence during those times I didn't know whether I was dead or alive. But that night, after the Italian restaurant, I didn't converse with them. I sat on a bench overlooking the gated private garden in Fitzroy Square in silence. I tilted my yellow fedora, my full moon in London's clouded night, and folded my arms. The absence of human presence became so prominent that the slightest touch of an idea left a mark. Just then, a thought came to me: maybe the fantasies we dream about most happen if we dream them out loud. I roared my longing for Bina-Balozi's skin at the top of my voice. I awakened Borges from his sleep. He huffed and puffed as he arrived at my bench, accompanied by his black and white cats. His mood was reflected in the poem he scrawled in the shadow of the moon on my head. In it, Borges promised that if he could live again, in the next life he'd try to make more mistakes, to be imperfect, less hygienic, to take more risks, make more trips, watch more sunsets, climb more mountains, have more real problems and fewer imaginary ones. I was about to pen my own poem, wishing the opposite to Borges, when I heard Bina-B's voice: Hannah? He said my name as if Lorca were camped out on the tip of his tongue while composing his poems about wine, transience, love, travel and duende. How did you know I was here? I asked him. I followed your fedora, he said. The fedora I wore not to veil myself from the world but to conceal myself from its interpretations of me. It poured. Bina-B opened his umbrella. Behind him, the pink roses of the gated Fitzroy Square Garden swayed. My eyes swooped to his lips as if taking an evening promenade on the bank of his breeze-filled mouth. O. Bina-B. BB stepped forward. Hannah, here. He offered me his umbrella. I declined. It's you who makes me wet, I wanted to tell him as I examined his face under the streetlamp's light. He was as smooth as the night, free of bitter thoughts. His plump lips and exfoliated skin, his eyes kohled by the charcoals mined from my dark thoughts, his cheekbones like summer birds about to fly with him through the black rain. Bina-Balozi stretched his arm and raised the umbrella further. The dark slim-fitting suit he wore to our date imprisoned his bones, and I imagined my fingers like mowers freeing his body to my hunger, his flesh to the invasion of my mind. My thoughts were running amok inside my head on this night of lust, when Bina-B coughed, then talked: Hannah, I want this but it's not easy. I pulled up the collar of my trench coat and lit a cigarette. I took a long drag and watched the rain. Hannah, do you understand me? BB asked. We spend a lifetime trying to conform to ideas handed down to us, I wanted to say to him. Let's instead build our own reality that reflects the ideas we birth in our imaginations – because imaginations are genderless wombs. Instead, I said, Bina-B, the time for explanation is over for me. I have nothing to add to the struggle. I flicked the cigarette butt on the ground. The wind brought the screeching of cars, the distant barking of dogs and the sirens of police cars. The sound of a city in conflict with itself reminded me of my own conflicts in the past. Bina-B paced up and down. He seemed like an orchestra without instruments, a city without people, a river without fish. I longed to enter him and anchor myself inside him like a bookmark inside a book. We lived in the shadow of exile, in the shadow of empty promises, in homes made of cardboard tents, in nations drawn on sand: peace, future, made sense only in our heads. Come to me, BB, I mumbled. Come. I was getting ahead of myself, my passion like a fast car speeding with me through this new terrain. Intoxicated by his gasps, I was out of control. For a second, I wanted to wrap him in my arms, to inveigle him into opening his body to my ravenousness. Then, and after a moment of calm, I sought to persuade him gently instead, to guide him to this moment with care, show him that if I could penetrate him, I would find a forgotten world inside him that he could then see mirrored in my eyes. But in truth, it felt as if our souls had already touched on the waiting lanes refugees go through in this country, that he and I had rubbed shoulders in the files at the Home Office containing our stories: where we lay naked of meaning and dignity, broken, adrift, not here nor there. Yes, I thought. We did cross paths and held hands, touching each other through our stories. No persuading was needed. I ached to know him as he lived back home, not carrying a tale of an immigrant but a boy growing up to be a man with the qualities of his mother. The trees on Fitzroy Square creaked and groaned, a choir as exquisite as the voice of an Eritrean praise singer. BB's shadow was thrown against the buildings overlooking the square as if he was part of the Victorian architecture. It struck me how I had likened all my lovers to lands, to places, as if my search for home had eroded the boundaries between my body and a country, so that the two had merged to make sense only when my desires were fully intact and in action. I extended my arm towards BB to bring him to me, to end my quest once and for all. Bina-B looked at me in silence. My thoughts intensified: why can't we love without questions, why do I have to convince him that our desires are as beautiful as our skin colour, why do I have to coax him to my thighs as if I were a hunter? Even the way we want to love has to be negotiated in the same way we sought asylum in this country, our fate hanging on a matter of believability. Yet what is there to believe or not to believe about us – two immigrants standing here in the heart of Bloomsbury, in the depth of the night, pretending that we're a myth. The rain beat down. Water dripped through the holes in the fabric of BB's umbrella. His face soaked, he asked me: Who are you? Hannah, I said. I'm sure he didn't see my smirk. Otherwise, he wouldn't have come closer to stimulate my appetite with the loss in his eyes. I met you once at Diana's, he said. Then a few times after that, and I heard. He paused. You heard what, Bina-B? That I lost my mind? That people saw me debating poetry with dead poets under my tree in Tavistock Square as if my chest was the Poets' Corner in Westminster Abbey? That I was in prison? That my selfishness drove a woman to her death? BB tightened his grip on his umbrella. Rain threw its curtains of black beads around him. He vanished, as if everything that had happened was a scene conceived in my mind, dreaming of a transcendental connection. ኩሉ ይሓልፍ ፍቅሪ ትቕጽል – *kullu yihalif, fiqri yiterif* – *everything passes, love remains*.

It was sunny on the day I departed Keren for London. But there was no change to the weather inside me. The mountains on which the Italians lost their battle and where their apartheid crumbled under the British feet bulged like haunted graves. This history, as steep as these mountains, would be mine to carry into my exile. My aunt stood next to me and tightened a scarf around her waist. As her shadow lengthened over the brown, dusty ground covered with stones, I understood she used the scarf to stop her wounds from breaking her in two. I peeled my eyes from her silhouette, storing a tall, whole and mighty version of her in my memory. A donkey rode another on the slope of the mountain opposite our veranda. The receiving donkey continued to chew the grass, undisturbed by the large weapon rummaging inside her from behind, her back unperturbed, her posture undiminished. That, my aunt told me, is a metaphor for life. You must take it in your stride no matter how hard you are screwed. I registered this episode in my mind, and it became as essential as the clothes I packed for the journey ahead to a land that, as I'd discover, embraced a similar mantra, which I exhorted to Bina-B on the bench of Fitzroy Square: O B. B., let's keep calm and carry on. My aunt clasped her arms around me and sang: *Hannah, the path ahead is dangerous / your heart must have teeth / your heart must have teeth*. That night, I was sent away from Keren to the country of the general who called my grandfather nigger. I'm sorry to send you to that country, my aunt said. But you have our stories inside you, and every story is like a lion. My aunt scraped together money from relatives and used the inheritance left by my parents and grandparents to pay the Eritrean smuggler, who coordinated with other smugglers to plan my journey to the UK, a journey that would take months. My aunt made me wear one of her outfits, a yellow cotton dress with a wide hem. ኩሉ ይሓልፍ ፍቅሪ ትቅጽል – *kullu yihalif, fiqri yiterif – everything passes, love remains*. And when I rode the smugglers' camel that evening in the Keren valley, it was as if the ground split open. I tumbled down the pit, my yellow dress like a deflated parachute speeding through the fall as I trekked from one country to another, through the desert, bushes, mountains, hungry and angry men, and the clouds. ኩሉ ይሓልፍ ፍቅሪ

ተቅጽል – *kullu yihalif, fiqri yiterif* – everything passes, love remains. When I arrived in Europe, as well as my family's and our country's fury against the British, my heart was also filled with rage at the men from my continent. The history of colonies etched on a mind inside a body brutalised at the hands of my fellow Africans. London threatened to become a saviour when the plane I was on sailed through the clouds and glided over its sky, the sky I would tell my story to, the sky big enough to contain words and secrets in its roving clouds. I peered at a city stretched out over a river, canals and hills. High on optimism, I was imagining my new life in my new city when I remembered what I had to do before landing, as instructed by my Egyptian smuggler in Cairo. I trod to the toilet with my bag. I ripped up the fake Egyptian passport that had enabled me to sneak through customs in Cairo and flushed it down the toilet, and with it the weight of deception that would get me to a safe place. I returned to my seat. The plane landed, and soon after I found myself standing in front of a customs officer. Our eyes met, and when he snickered I was seized by the memory of my grandfather's encounter with the British general at the foot of the Keren mountains. The officer leant back into his chair and the light on the wall behind him highlighted his ironic expression. My impressions about English people for a long time were set in those minutes as I faced this man at the entry gate, whose face tightened as he studied me. Hello, passport? he asked. I froze. He tapped his desk with his index finger. I remembered the piece of paper written in English given to me by my Egyptian smuggler. I had learnt English in school and by reading my father's books, some of which were in English, but my smuggler instructed me to pretend

I couldn't speak it. Although their empire had collapsed
a long time ago, my smuggler said, they still like to feel
superior. It will help your case if you look ignorant in front
of them. I bowed my head and said: Me English no speak.
I reached into my top pocket and gave it to him. It said in
capital letters: I SPEAK TIGRINYA, AMHARIC AND ARABIC.
I DON'T HAVE A PASSPORT. I AM FROM ERITREA, FLEEING
WAR, AND I AM HERE TO SEEK ASYLUM. He read it, shook
his head and picked up the phone. I wheezed. Water, I asked
in Tigrinya. What? the officer asked. Water, please, I said in
Arabic, and when he enquired again, I asked it in Amharic,
in Tigre, in all the languages I spoke, except English. Water.
Please. Three uniformed men drove me out of the airport in
a passenger van. I entered London begging for water. Water,
please. The car drove so fast that the streetlamps and trees
were swallowed by the speed. The dryness in my throat
deepened as if the drought of the desert had followed me
to this island. The van jolted over consecutive speed bumps.
I asked the driver for water. He put the stereo on. My belly
growled. Water, I mumbled. Water. When we reached the
destination, the building, enclosed with fences topped with
barbed wire, reminded me of the Ethiopian army prison
back home. The corridor, though, smelt like a hospital. I no
sick, I said to the men. I refugee look home safe. You what?
I no hospital need. Need a safe country only. He said something that I missed. Listen, I said to the men in English.
What? one of them asked. I repeated it, this time letter by
letter, L-i-s-t-e-n. The man shook his head. In this country,
we say *lisen*, he said. I wondered about the missing letter T
and why they decided to throw it away – and as if I developed
instant kinship with a letter ejected from its rightful place,
I gave the T a home on my tongue and enunciated each

letter slowly: *listen*. And as I trailed the two men hurtling down the corridor, thirsty, hungry and breathless, my bag against my chest, I surrendered to the thought of being caught in webs of diseases. I was invigorated by an absurd notion that health had no purpose for me anymore – I think I even smiled with bewilderment. The men took me to a small room with a single bed and a square, white coffee table. An officer signed with his hands and asked if I wanted to eat. I shook my head. I needed water, which I drank in one gulp when it came. Questions filled my head, some as bland as the toilet's whereabouts, others variations of the primary thought that had been occupying my mind: what will happen to me now? I paced around the room. I took off my shoes but put them on again. I staggered around the room, imagining being tortured for carrying a fake passport. I sat slumped against the wall, my arms around my bag, which contained my mother's diary, a couple of changes of clothes and my aunt's yellow dress, ripped apart by men in the desert. The door opened. A man signed with his hand to get up. I smelt coffee on his breath. As if I could drink it from the air, I inhaled and jumped to my feet. He took me to a large office, exchanged words with a black man and a white man sitting around a long brown conference table, and left. The men wore similar suits. And I had dreaded men in identical clothing ever since what had happened in our hometown by the streetlamp and in the desert on the way to this country. I stood still by the door. Come on in, said one of the two men. He ran his hand through his grey hair. When I didn't move, he pointed at the chair. Take a seat, he said. The other, stocky and with a thin moustache, followed me with his eyes as I sat on a chair. A few portraits of men and women hung on the white walls. There was a pile of newspapers at one end of the table. A woman in a rain jacket and a red bag dashed through the door. Sorry I'm late, she said, as she shook the men's hands. The rain in her hair fell onto my face as she turned towards me. London raindrops stroked my cheek and tears filled my eyes. The woman greeted me in Arabic. Sorry, they couldn't find a Tigrinya speaker, but I was told you spoke Arabic too, she said. OK. She took the chair to my right, between the men and me. They talked in English, so fast that I couldn't follow everything. She turned to me and said, Hannah, they've given me a few questions to ask you, and it's in your best interest if you tell the truth. OK. They'll write all your answers on this form. She pointed to a pile of paper in front of the moustached man. This is a basic application form. You'll get to fill in the main one with a lawyer. The first question is, what's your full name? Hannah Xehay. How old are you? Seventeen. How can you prove this? What do you mean? Well, Hannah, if you don't have your passport, how can the authorities confirm you're seventeen? I shrugged. Hannah, if you don't show them proof, they might assume you're an adult, and they'll keep you in this place until they discover the truth somehow. I have no evidence, I said. Alright, let's move on. Where did you come from? Eritrea. Why did you come to ask for asylum? Well, it wasn't my choice. Whose choice was it? My aunt's. Why did she send you to this country? She didn't say much. She mentioned things to do with living in this country. Like what? the interpreter asked. Safety, I said. And education. As requested by the interpreter, I revealed to her some of the details of my journey to get here. I told her that the desert had mountains made of African bones, which she felt was too dramatic to translate. I then told her that I came close to being killed a few times. But all that didn't matter to my application. Alright, Hannah, but let me go back to what your aunt said. Did she tell you why you couldn't find safety and education in Sudan or Egypt? No. Do you know why? How would I know? Alright, do you have any siblings? No. Alright. Is there a doctor here? I asked her. Where do you have pain? All over, I said, but especially my head. Is it a headache? No, it's just full of things I can't stop thinking about. She translated what I said to the men, and what they said to me. Hannah, organising a psychologist would take time, and I'm sorry, but we'll have to continue with the interview. OK, I said. Hannah, we have questions about your passport, she said. My stomach churned. I spat on the floor. One of the men, and I can't remember which, wagged his finger: Disgusting. No spitting here. His colleague patted his back. Thank you, I'm OK, he said. But I no OK, I said, in English. I no OK. But the interpreter continued: Hannah, I need to ask you about your passport. If you wish, I said, and massaged my forehead. Where's your passport? I cut it up and flushed it down the plane's toilet. Why? The smuggler told me to do so. Do you know what your smuggler looked like? I thought about her question. He had brown skin, but his behaviour was like theirs, I said, pointing at the Englishmen in front of us. Hannah, I won't be translating this for your own good, she said. As you wish, but it's the truth, I said. She turned to the men and engaged them in a conversation at a speed I didn't understand. After a while, she said to me: Hannah, they'll transfer you to an organisation that helps find accommodation for minor refugees. I guess they'll try to place you with a foster carer, and you'll be assigned a lawyer to help you file your application to the Home Office. She explained what each detail meant, and

I had to stop her after a while. I have no space in my head, I said. Hannah, she said. This is the beginning. Please take care. I find your warning strange, I said. If I don't have a space in my head, I don't. You're not the first immigrant who's told me this, she said. Don't let memories overpower you. But don't worry, you'll learn to let go of the past. That's the only way. ኩሉ ይሓልፍ ፍቅሪ ትቅጽል – *kullu yihalif, fiqri yiterif – everything passes, love remains.* O. B. B. How could I have known at that detention centre that I'd empty a large section of the shelves of my memory to stock my moments with Bina-B? I remember I bought my strap-on the morning after I bumped into BB at a friend's house party. Wearing a vintage floral shirt and brown trousers, BB was kissing a woman, who stood against a wall, her arms lifeless. He wiggled his hips as he arched his back, pushing his bottom out, delivering his chest and neck to her mouth, which remained sealed. Everything about him called to be conquered, to be led, to be ravaged. The sight of this lascivious creature in such restrained company so incensed me that I set out on pulling him away from his girlfriend, step by step. I invited them both to supper at my studio flat for the following week, but that night, after I had returned to my studio in Great Portland Street, I couldn't sleep. I sat in my bed and thought about him. I rented my studio from an old Greek man who owned the fish and chip joint I'd frequented for years. One day he sold his business and returned to his hometown to be closer to the sea. We all need a sea, he told me. My sea, I said, is a memory that blows into my thoughts an atmosphere of sorrow. And that makes me happy. The Greek man asked me if I wanted to sublet his studio at a discounted rate. Because, he said, I know you'll look after it the way you looked after the Keren mountains in your heart through all these years of exile. When I held the door of the studio apartment open for Bina-B and his girlfriend, she entered and looked around. But BB's focus stayed on me. I beamed. I didn't want a lover who would marvel at the decor of my studio and throw meaningless pleasantries around, applauding my taste. BB fixed his attention on my eyes, as if they were the gateway to the rooms inside me, rooms I had adorned with my bitter experiences, lust, lies and truths, rooms where I fucked and was fucked, rooms where I cried for help only to hear the echo of my loneliness gathering depth in the corners. And as I expected him to be, Bina was swept away by the details of the rooms he could glimpse through my eyes. He came closer to inspect what I had decorated my interiors with over the years. I wondered if he'd seen my mother's diary, which I'd placed in the same room as my father's shrine. I drew him even closer to her words and to that moment when I'd left the detention centre with the Arabic interpreter's words about immigrants succumbing to the weight of memories ringing in my ears. Outside the detention centre on my first day in London, trees touched as if in an embrace. Plants climbed on buildings with colourful doors and windows. The interpreter said the government couldn't provide me with therapy anytime soon and I'd have to wait years for my application to be processed first, but I found consolation in the London air drifting into the car that drove me to the aid organisation. Flocks of green birds flew out of a park as our car sped past. A song came on the radio that was so repetitive that parts of it were easy to remember: *I'd give it all up for you / I'd give it all up for you / I'd give it all up for you.* We arrived at our destination. They handed me to a refugee organisation as if I were a crumpled, dog-eared book that

everyone had attempted to read before stopping midway
through, having stumbled across difficult sentences,
disturbing images, and then quitting and passing me on.
I found myself in a reader's hands full of germs. My chest
heavy, I sat on a chair, back folded, elbows on knees.
Everything will be fine, the receptionist said as she handed
me a glass of water. Doors opened here and there. Personnel
exited the offices and scattered around the reception area.
They disappeared back inside their offices without a glance
at me after speaking with the receptionist or fetching
beverages from a kitchen at the far end of the corridor. When
one of them turned his head in my direction, I stood up.
But as time passed and he continued to stare, I gathered he
was looking through me. It was as if losing home had made
me invisible. I asked the receptionist if she had a mirror.
She took one from her make-up purse. I gasped on seeing
myself: it was as if, rather than my own face, I was looking
at someone I had come across in passing many years before.
I struggled to comprehend the changes that had taken place
in the few months since I had left Keren – my features
gathered dust, memories like a sandstorm obscuring them.
I blew over the mirror, examined my reflection again, and
observed the absence of dreams in my eyes, and the presence of emptiness. I hadn't slept for weeks, and I was meant
to tell them a story to persuade them of my right to live in
their country, but weren't my wounds as visible as the fish
in the pond on the portrait hanging on the reception wall?
I envied the coloured plasters on the receptionist's elbow.
I'd cover my body head to toe with hundreds of coloured
plasters if I could. I handed the receptionist her mirror and
sat back on the chair. A man in blue overalls and wearing
yellow rubber gloves burst through the door, rolling a mop

in a bucket. The smell of bleach hung in the air long after he passed. A group of staff arrived carrying files. As they chatted among themselves, I searched their faces for clues about my situation. But many donned a mask of the kind I had first noticed at the airport, and then at the detention centre. Was this something Eritreans and English people had in common or something else they'd looted from us along with much of our country's wealth? I was thinking about our shared attributes with the English and regretting the way we had chosen to camouflage our emotions and feelings in this way when a far darker thought about them crossed my mind. Perhaps they chose not to see me. Perhaps their way of finding peace with their history was to bury the past and me in it. Otherwise, they would have seen that I was a consequence of a tragedy their country had manufactured when they annexed Eritrea to Ethiopia. Yet here I was in London trying to convince them of the legitimacy of my story and my case for asylum. Keys jingled in pockets and my eyes rolled as a coin rattled on the floor. Noises everywhere. Footsteps, heavy footsteps, quick footsteps, hurried footsteps. The whistles and the phone. Fweet phwwwwwhht Fweet phwwwwwhht. Treeerrree. Treeerrree phwwwwwhht Fweet phwwwwwhht Treeerrree. Treeerrree phwwwwwhht. I covered my ears. I remember thinking I was in a factory where human stories were processed, I remember thinking of the people whose stories the staff carried in folders, I remember seeing a man in an orange T-shirt with sweaty armpit marks carrying a box with files and I remember thinking about how heavy our stories were, I remember a woman in a sari rushing down the hallway with a stack of papers in her arms, I remember a bald, bespectacled man with haggard eyes holding a large cup of coffee. He was the one who found me accommodation with someone named Diana Omario. ኩሉ ይሓልፍ ፍቅሪ ትቅጽል – *kullu yihalif, fiqri yiterif* – *everything passes, love remains*. At the memory of Diana on that bench in Fitzroy Square, I lit a cigarette. Bina-B called my name. I didn't respond. I turned my attention to the bench I was sitting on. Like the many benches I used over the years when I lived in the streets, it was made of thick pieces of rot-resistant wood to withstand decades of high-traffic usage and repel insects and mould, but was it sturdy enough to survive my carnality, the germs of my passion, and what I had envisaged doing to Bina-B? I smiled. In the silence that followed on that night in Fitzroy Square, in the presence of Bina-B, the more I thought of my story, the more I revealed of myself. Words, like torch beams, illuminated my reality in a different way. Behind Bina-B, in the distance, a cyclist pedalled through the rain, in the way Bina-B and I plodded our way to something both of us wanted. BB swung around and gave his back to my lust. O B.B. As his eyes roamed over the gated garden, I wondered about the garden inside him. After a moment, he turned towards me and said, Hannah, I feel that you, me, Anne and all the underage immigrants who have been at Diana's house played a role in her death. ኩሉ ይሓልፍ ፍቅሪ ትቅጽል – *kullu yihalif, fiqri yiterif* – *everything passes, love remains... EYES: Hannah exits Tavistock Square... tyres screech... dogs bark... birds chirp... pigeons coo... police sirens... laughter from a Spanish throat... swearing in English... sexy words in Swahili... fingers poking nostrils... spit falling on the pavements like hail... music in Arabic ... enter the sun... harsh... sweaty foreheads everywhere... hot... really hot... c'est chaud... what do you expect... the sun gets upset... gives the finger as it climbs a cloud and disappears... the wind picks up... Hannah hears its laughter... phew... it's cold... this*

English weather... rain falls... people rushing everywhere... dreams falling on the floor with the coins... click-clack... clack-click... a black cat born in Paris smuggled to London via Brussels strolls over and picks a few of the dreams to do with sex and laughs so hard at some of the perverted Londoners carrying fantasies while strait-jacketed in respectability... she laughs... c'est une forme de servitude c'est... go back to where you came from a London cat yells... the Parisian cat ignores the abuse and heads to Tavistock Square to discuss illusion with Borges's black and white cats resting on the autumn leaves of Hannah's tree... the day is over and night falls... the moon plays hide and seek with London before finally appearing in parts... its light is unnecessary because London glows from within... and the moon becoming a metaphor is not good for anybody so it vanishes... leaving behind a reminder in the glint in Hannah's eyes looking at a parked car... and through its window at lips licking a dick... and the blow job is over when a gag reflex kicks in... but the man wants another round... so he stands on his knees on the driver's seat of his car... his bottom round and firm and pressing against the window... Hannah's heart jolts... fuck what a nice ass she yells... Diana lived in Kilburn, I was told by the refugee organisation's caseworker, a tall man in a red cap and a grey coat, as I sat in the back seat of his car. The caseworker put the radio on. I was on my way to a British person's home. I was on my way to a place to live. I was in. I was in. I was in, in, in. I cradled my bag on my lap and wound down the window. We drove past stores with signs that said 'House of Cards', 'Gifts' and 'Welcome'. I was in. We crossed a bridge over a river and the water beneath rose and fell. I was in. We came across a clock at the top of a long tower that I thought had the function of timing the clouds. I was in. We drove past a post office with a queue of people that stretched

around the block. I wanted to ask the driver to stop so
I could send a letter to my aunt to tell her I was in, when
I remembered I had no address or telephone number.
ኩሉ ይሓልፍ ፍቅሪ ትቅጽል – *kullu yihalif, fiqri yiterif – everything
passes, love remains*. We turned into a side street. The air
seeped inside me. My cheeks puffed up to twice their size.
Spurred on by my impatience to smell, see and feel London,
I leant on the open window. London's clouds remained
static as the caseworker drove from one street to the next,
across junctions, traffic lights and roundabouts. I was in.
Our car jerked when it screeched to a halt in the traffic like
clothing caught on a door. I slammed my head on the seat
in front. I'm sorry, said the caseworker. I wasn't. I was the
closest I had ever been to Londoners on the pavements.
Some looked like me, but I also noticed a resemblance in
those who didn't share my physical appearance but surrendered to their thoughts in the way that I did. This common
thread among those who populated the footpath left me
conflicted. I had landed in a city suitable for my melancholia,
but the London my aunt had talked about was meant to be
ecstatic. I had fled a city in a war zone to another engaged in a
different kind of conflict, a city full of people in a fight with
their feelings and thoughts. People bumped into each other.
Sorry. Thank you. Excuse me. Pardon me. When I spotted
men sleeping on the streets in beds made of cardboard,
I thought the city was full and I was the last lucky one to
find a room in it. It drizzled. As I moved between sadness
and happiness, fear and elation, the car sped on. I was in,
in a new country and in a hurricane inside my head. I was
in. When my thoughts calmed, an item on the radio grabbed
my attention. The presenter talked in a slow and clear voice
that I could partly understand. He spoke about many people

being out of work. He reported on a bombing in London. And when the newsreader resumed a piece on mad cow disease the caseworker changed the channel. Our eyes met in the rear-view mirror. A caller in the live call-in swore. I caught *fuck... prices... high... fuck*. The radio host ended the call and apologised to listeners. He suggested the caller look outside his window and cheer up because the sun was out. I looked at the sky. Sun shone through the clouds for a while and then evanesced. We are here, the caseworker said. I took my aunt's yellow dress out of my bag and left it behind me on the car seat as if I could also let go of what had happened in the desert. ኩሉ ይሓልፍ ፍቅሪ ትቅጽል – *kullu yihalif, fiqri yiterif* – *everything passes, love remains*. I stepped out of the car on Kilburn High Road, the cold air assailed my skin. I shuddered. I remember thinking, on hearing people speaking the same language in different accents, that those people would be my people and this country would be my country and this weather would be my weather and that instead of lamenting my misfortune at being alone, I should be cheered by the possibility of gaining something new, even if it were something as small as a drop of rain sliding into the crack of my lips. When we walked under a bridge off Kilburn High Road to Diana's, I heard a cooing above my head. I looked up. Pigeons sat with fluffed feathers on steel beams. A giant blob of poop landed on my shoulder, which I was alerted to when Diana opened the door of her house, which looked like any of the other buildings on both sides of this tree-populated street, and said: Oh, you got pigeon shit on your jacket. She took a piece of tissue out of her jeans pocket. The caseworker chortled. Language, Diana, he said. She rolled her large brown eyes. It was like seeing my reflection in a mirror. She looked like me, I thought, as she tucked strands of her long curly hair behind her ears. She spread her arms as if to take me into an embrace when a sound behind me distracted her. Oh God, not you again, she mumbled. I looked back. A man leant out of the first-floor window of a three-storey building across the narrow street. He wore a blue blazer and a tie draped around his pink shirt. He stared at me in silence. But his poker face broke the longer he probed me. His face turned the colour of his shirt as if I were the tie around his neck. The man slammed the window shut. I remembered my aunt's story about the British officer who had screamed obscenities at my grandfather on what he thought was his day of freedom and a new beginning. Diana took me in her arms. The smell of rosemary and lemon sage wafted from her as if every pore on her neck contained a garden box. It's so lovely to meet you, Hannah, she said as she tightened her arms around me, giving me the impression that she too needed a home in me. I was on my way inside her house with that feeling of reciprocity when the man's window creaked open again. I jerked my head back and trembled. Come inside, Diana said. Once inside, before she signed a few papers with the refugee organisation's human courier, Diana inspected me. Perhaps she was looking for bruises to prevent accusations of abuse. There was nothing, nothing visible, nothing she could see yet. She took me in and placed my bag in the hallway. I'll introduce you to everyone, Diana said, speaking slowly. This everyone amounted to one other. Anne. Anne is at work now, Diana said, adding, Well, I think. Anne worked in a fast-food restaurant in Piccadilly Circus. The rest I hope Anne herself will fill you in on, Diana tittered. OK, sweetheart, let me show you around. The three-storey terraced house had four bedrooms. The living room, kitchen and toilet were downstairs. The living room had a small desk, a TV, a landline and a fireplace. Videos, newspapers and books were scattered on the floor around a three-seater cream fabric sofa. A high, white L-shaped shelf packed with books stood to the right of the fireplace. I edged towards it. My father had hidden all the books he'd collected and buried them to spare the words from ruin and to save them for future generations, but Diana exhibited her books. The covers of Diana's books came in different colours and designs. Writers whose names I recognised from the books my father saved were next to others I didn't know. Writers from different countries stood side by side in the same home as if to engage in conversations across cultures, time, gender and religion. I wished I could scale the shelf and slip myself between these books, those standing upright and those lying flat on their backs as if taking a well-deserved break from ruminating over life and its meaning. Do you like books? Diana asked me, slowly, and repeated every word to ensure I had understood. I nodded, and we moved on with the tour around her house. The dining room, kitchen and toilet were at the end of the hallway that led to the garden shed, where she kept the washing machine. Let's continue, she said as she proceeded ahead of me up the stairs to the rest of the house. I paused on the stairs at the gallery wall with framed pictures of Diana's parents. I had gathered from the way my father filled his bedroom with my mother's photos that pictures hold more than a reminder of the physical appearance of those who depart and that every image is a gateway to a memory, to a moment, a day, a year, a lifetime. The staircase held Diana's archives. On the first floor, there was Diana's room and a bathroom. Diana opened her room. The scent of roses and spices that circled in the air wafted inside me. I threw my arms wide open and gulped more of the fragranced air. Is everything alright, Hannah? Diana asked. I think I smiled. Or laughed. Diana's second floor was flooded with a cold wind. Diana leant a small ladder against the wall at the far end of the hallway. She climbed it and shut the door of the attic. After stepping off the ladder, she pointed at the two rooms with a bathroom in between. The one closer to the stairs was Anne's room. I'm afraid we can't go in, said Diana. There was a large sticker of a black panther on Anne's door. Unlike all the other doors, which were painted white, Anne's was dark green, giving the impression the black panther was emerging from a forest in pursuit of its prey. My chest pounded as I looked at Anne's choice of animal guarding her world and imagined the interior of her room. Diana spoke over my thoughts: Come, sweetheart. The panther's golden eyes stalked me as I tottered behind Diana to the opposite end of the corridor. This is your room, said Diana. Do not open it, I said to her. Diana turned towards me. Your English sounds better than I thought, she said. I speak little, I said. I asked for scissors. Why? Scissors, I said again. Let's go back to the bathroom, she said. When we did, I closed the door and chopped my hair. Oh god, Hannah, what have you done? Your beautiful curls. Why did you do that, Hannah? My window opened onto a view of a Jubilee line track. I peeked my head through it. The sky growled as two trains hurtled past each other on opposite lines. It was at Diana's that I fell in love with London rain in more than one way. I had for the first time noticed its many colours. Black when it fell on the rail track, becoming brighter and bluish as it broke into small particles under the probing light of the streetlamps. And it rained when I met Anne for the first time. On the evening of my first day at Diana's, I sat in my bed with my mother's diary and opened it, as if in need of a mother's wisdom to start me on my new life, for her words to moor me in this stranger's house in Kilburn. But as soon as I read the first entry, I closed it again. *Thursday. 11 p.m.: Some like their sex differently, and my new lover, Xehay, understands that my desires lie in what many consider horrific and disgusting. My light comes from a dark place. I admire how he accepts himself to be the recipient of such love, even if it's painful, but then again, he loves pain. His satisfaction comes when he crosses the threshold of normality. Oh, we're going to have so much fun together. Our needs and desires are so complementary.* It was as if I'd swallowed bones, her words trapped in my throat. I buried the diary under my bed sheet and rushed to the window. A train sped by, lurching as it travelled along the rail, but even the screech of its wheels couldn't drown my mother's voice inside my head. She sounded different in her own words from the way I had imagined her to be. My image of her was constructed through my father's memories. I remember that night my father stood in the middle of the room with her portrait in his arms next to an oil lamp, or the evenings he'd have his supper in our garden with my mother's portrait on a chair opposite him, the table scattered with red roses. Some nights he'd sit in our garden in his suit with his glass of tej wine, his eyes fixed on the sky, as if following her evening promenade among the stars. He gave me the impression that my mother was as romantic as him. Meeting her in her diary convinced me that the version of her in my father's head was something he had created. I couldn't get my mother out of my mind. A deluge started. Scent of the rail track, which Diana told me was creosote, wafted into my room along with the rhythm of its relentless beatings as the trains raced along both sides. I was about to snuggle into my bed next to my mother's diary when the voice of someone who hated rain with the same intensity as I loved it blasted through the door of my room. For fuck's sake, I'm fucking wet. It must be Anne, I thought. She sounded husky, as if she spoke through a throat filled with desires. I opened the door ajar. The smell of chips drifted to my nostrils. Her skin burst through her soaked white dress. Her square face with a chiselled jawline made her look athletic and as fierce as the black panther on her door. Her eyes under thick eyebrows were narrow and dark. London summer rain dripped from her long, silky hair. What the fuck are you looking at? she asked. I slammed the door and leant against it. Her voice reverberated in my head. My breasts hardened, my nipples like rockets about to soar with me. Music blasted from her room. I exited my room and tiptoed to hers, to the black panther on the door, to the male singers vowing to spill their passion on one single night. I caught some of the lyrics, which I later sang to Bina-B as I slipped my hands under his suit in the gated gardens of Fitzroy Square, the night breeze filling the paws of the beast in me: *Let me… / lick you up… / … Let me play with your… / Baby… / I wanna be… man.* I can't remember when I started to be attracted to rage, finding pleasure in violence. I have no story to tell about coming to terms with it. The first story I ever had to be reconciled to was my asylum application to the Home Office, which I submitted via my British-Asian lawyer and her British-Eritrean assistant, a bald man with a soul patch. After I recounted my story, the lawyer noted it down and read what she had written on the application form. You took out most of what I told you about why I fled, I said. The lawyer reassured me: Every officer at the Home Office is looking for reasons to reject an application, so we just adjusted the story to give it a better chance of succeeding. I didn't understand. But everything I told you is the truth, I said. I know, said the lawyer. And we believe you, Hannah, but please trust that we speak from experience. The Home Office is populated by people and not machines. And we need to find subtle ways to appeal to their emotions. The British-Eritrean man mentioned facts about my family I had told them. Hannah, he said, think about what happened to your mother and father, and you'll understand why it's important to ensure your application is successful. I thought about the success and failure of a story and how it depends on other factors beyond the truth. The lawyer confirmed this thought to me when she said: Hannah, you're trying to join another country, another culture. We aim to introduce your story in ways it won't offend. OK? I shook my head. I wasn't making anything up. What I told them about the British was also in the books I'd read. I'm here because the British annexed my country to Ethiopia and that led to the war I fled, I said, emphasising a fact I'd already mentioned. My father would never forgive me if I didn't put all of this in my story. The lawyer intertwined her fingers and placed her hands on my application on her desk. Hannah, you don't have to do it if you don't want to, she said. But you have to decide now, we can't have this back and forth. I remembered how my father's face lit up whenever he gave me a book to read before he buried it, as if he were constructing a library of knowledge inside me. I pleaded with the lawyer and her assistant to leave my story the way it was. An asylum application is not, let me repeat, is not about the past, the lawyer said. I finally understood: to live in peace, I had to live blind to my past.

They told me about the tolerance that made this country the best in the world. Look at us in this room now, the lawyer said. Would this happen anywhere else? That room, though, suffocated me. Who are we, I thought, if our stories have to be changed, amended and simplified in order to live in peace? Can't you see the contradiction? I asked my lawyer. Of what, Hannah? Of being asked to live a false version of myself in a free country, I said. The lawyer and her assistant exchanged a stare. I want to live with my wounds as well as my rage against what this country has done to my grandfather and his people, I said. Then don't come to ask for asylum here, said the Eritrean assistant. You should go to Italy. Giving the atrocities they committed against our people, surely there you'll find a better axe to grind. I stood up. Are you going to Italy? he asked. The lawyer tapped his arm. OK, he said. I'm sorry. Hannah, please sit. I think in time you'll learn to balance your views. Our country's not perfect, but it's special. Silence. Then: I think it's time we moved on, the lawyer said. OK? I closed my eyes. ኩሉ ይሓልፍ ፍቕሪ ትቕጽል – *kullu yihalif, fiqri yiterif* – *everything passes, love remains*. I'm ready, I said. Great, let's crack on then, said the assistant. I had to be open and get every detail right. They recorded my height and weight, the colour of my eyes and hair, the details of my past life in Eritrea, what I knew of my parents' personal history, as well as the route of my trip to Great Britain, the smugglers' names, which I invented since I couldn't or didn't want to remember, and their modus operandi, as if I would know, as well as the reasons for my application and who had paid for me to make the expensive escape from a war zone. They softened the rough edges of my story, cut out the controversial bits and homed in on the present atrocities between African nations that led me to flee, leaving out the inconvenient truths of the contributing factors of world order, disentangling me from my reality and creating a simple, presentable version of a refugee who would fit into the future of this country. I was boxed as Black African, woman, straight. I thought about what would happen if my application was turned down. I couldn't imagine leaving my story behind. I thought of those who had been deported but whose stories remained with the Home Office. I wanted to ask my lawyer about this, but I didn't. As I signed the application form, I felt the opposite of free. My story was submitted and I had to wait. Cross your fingers, they told me. What do you mean? Well, it's you and your luck, the lawyer said. A story's not science. You'll succeed if your story comes across the desk of someone who finds it convincing. Otherwise, you won't. So, I waited. In the meantime, I started to get to know Diana and to get closer to Anne without ever getting to know her. Anne and I encountered each other by night. Here in Kilburn, north-west London, in the heart of the night, I started to carve out my own story, full of terror and beauty. This story would belong to me alone, until that night in Fitzroy Square when I shared it with Bina-Balozi. O Bina-B. *O* for the rose between his black cheeks, *B* for the ballet dancer on the floor of my lap. O BB, I need to pee, I said. There's a bar around the corner, he said. I gaped at his lips, thick and full at the centre like a runway for my thighs – give me your mouth, I wanted to tell him. Otherwise, you can go to your place and I'll wait for you here, he said. No, I said, reminding him of my time under my tree in Tavistock Square... *EYES: Hannah wakes up... looks up at the sky and sees the sun bursting through the clouds as though it's the anus of the universe... this image sets her mood: she's caught between*

*optimism and gloom... someone in the park announces that it's
a bank holiday Monday... she leans against her tree... people
march up and down... picture here, there and over there... smile...
say cheese... how do I look?... come on take another one just for
posterity's sake... the wind blows the long ponytail of a bald man
in a suede jacket... a man and a woman enter the park chatting...
yet there's a distance between them... mind the gap Hannah
wants to tell them but her attention drifts to a pigeon that strides
ahead of her holding a flower in its beak... Hannah tiptoes behind
the pigeon... the pigeon offers its flowering beak to another pigeon...
the two rub their beaks together and coo as they retreat behind
Hannah's tree... evening arrives... people go home... Hannah
lies down on her back... the pigeons are still behind her tree...
a man walks in in a green cardigan and green trousers as if to
be camouflaged in the park... Hannah wonders what he's hiding...
she tenses... alert she stands up and grabs her bag... the man stops
near a tree at the opposite end of the park... then turns in Hannah's
direction... he unzips his trousers and swings his dick out...* Back
at Diana's, it was close to nine in the evening and Diana sat
in the living room watching the evening news. I fetched a
book from the shelf and sat next to her. I wasn't allowed by
the government to study or work, and I ate with the money
the Department of Social Security paid me via Diana, who
used some of it to buy shopping and gave the rest of it to me
as pocket money. Diana turned the TV off and read with me.
The front door creaked. Scent of fries rushed through my
body. Diana scurried to the kitchen, and moments later she
called me over. Look at what Anne brought for us, she said.
Here, take the fries and burger. I'll put the ice cream in the
fridge. I remember how everyone said thank you and how
that made me uncomfortable to eat without saying a thank
you to Anne. I was about to do so when Diana stopped me.

Don't worry about it, leave her alone for now, sweetheart.
I wanted to ask why, but I continued with my dinner.
I thought of Anne behind the black panther-guarded green door. My thoughts about her glowed in the light of her absence. Her occasional tenderness was like a distant light that didn't deflect from her dark side, and I longed to submerge myself in her darkness. On my way to my room after eating the burger and chips, I paused by Anne's door and was about to knock when it seemed to me the black panther scrunched its face and snarled at me. I shuddered at what I felt I had seen and hastened to my room. I turned around. Anne played her song. *You, you, you, you... / let me freak you / You, you, you...* I'd sometimes walk around my room, thinking here, while sat on the chair, there at my study desk, and over there by the window. These thoughts penetrated my head as I looked at Bina-B, who stood still by the gates of Fitzroy Square gardens. From my room at Diana's house, London gave wings to thoughts that flew me closer to absurdity. I needed a knee on my chest, hands on my arms to pin me to reality in my new milieu, and fantasising about Anne, a Londoner, became the magnet that pulled me towards London, a city whose charms, no matter how hidden and mysterious they remained, I could find in Anne's eyes. One night, which came on the back of another idle day wasted while waiting for the Home Office decision on my application, I stood by my window and stared at the sky. The lure of joining my parents for a stroll among the stars was so strong that I couldn't push it away. Just then, Anne came to the fore of my mind. She stirred my senses. I gave in to the thought of her, to being pulled by her imaginary presence. I dug my nails into my skin so deep that I slept that night and many of the nights that

followed with open wounds through which there seeped more wild ideas. One night, as the Jubilee trains bolted in both directions past my window and the sirens drifted in and out of earshot, I turned my attention to the room, which had been occupied by Bina-Balozi before he left sometime before my arrival. It had a wooden floor, its walls decorated with pictures of seas and rivers chosen by Bina-Balozi. It was his idea, too, Diana told me, to have the wall against the bed painted in dusky lilac. I met Bina-Balozi's style and sensibilities before sampling his inner splendour in Fitzroy Square. O Bina-B. My wardrobe was still empty as I lived out of my bag, ready to be deported if my application was rejected. I had yet to use the black wooden desk with a chair that Diana had bought for me. An alarm clock was on top of the desk. It was 10 a.m., the date I can't remember. I remember, though, those evenings in the living room reading Diana's books and watching TV with her and thinking about why there were no black people in the soap operas, I remember asking Diana whether that was because there were not many black actors, I remember her smiling and saying, Let's not talk about that, sweetheart, I remember the songs I watched on *Top of the Pops*, and I remember telling Diana how much I wanted to dress like one of the singers, who glided onto the stage with red hair and wearing a leather corset, bright, tight trousers and boots. I memorised some of his songs. I remember humming one of his songs as I made a pair of shorts out of trousers, added patches to my jeans and rearranged the clothes I had to suit the person I was becoming, planting my transition into a new entity with the help of music and the guidance of musicians. My spoken English improved so fast that Diana said I talked as if I'd lived in London for years already. Her words encouraged me to venture out of the house. One morning, when a rainbow adorned the sky like a necklace, I opened the door and instinctively raised my eyes towards the opposite building. The man stood by his window holding a book. But as he glared at me, I wondered how a book could dim the light of his eyes. In my room, I sat on my bed with my mother's diary. Her diary had no dates. It was anchored to moments, thoughts, as if her short time on this earth was bound not to time but to the intensity with which she lived out her feelings. I flipped a few pages and started reading. *Wednesday. 1 a.m.: I first saw Xehay in the dry riverbed a few weeks ago. He was alone, facing the Keren mountains that seemed as old as his soul. In the way he stood – tall and firm – he looked like an acacia tree. Yet he also seemed distracted. His hair blew in all directions as the breeze flashed by. He had a stick in his hand, which made me think he might be a shepherd, but no animals were around him. He was alone, and he waved the stick in the air as if to shepherd his thoughts. The contradictions I observed drew me to him: he needed a type of love to soothe him, break him apart, glue him together again. The idea of dismantling and assembling him stirred me. I whistled. He turned and froze, staring at me in silence. Ha. My mother constantly reassures our relatives, wearied by my personality, that I have a heart under my austere demeanour, but I only felt it now when my chest quivered as I scrutinised Xehay. It was as if we had met in our dreams and crossed paths in the depths of the night. As if we had recognised each other from a previous life where we were separated by rules and traditions. But I now felt the ruler of this terrain. I beckoned him towards me. He came and stood without saying anything. Days later, he dropped by my feet. He loves the taste of our land on my soles, and he reveres the freedom I hid from the colonisers between my toes.* I threw the diary on the floor and put a pillow over my head. I curled my body and pressed my knees against my stomach. Her absence from my life since I was a baby ordained her with such power that the slightest encounter with her words in her diary was enough for her writing to possess me. I waited all this time for something that would make her existence more concrete than just as a mother who gave birth to me and then died. The diary was where she sought sanctuary from her grave and reincarnated herself in her own words. I could see and feel her. This thought came to me as my longing for a mother's presence in my life impelled me towards her diary, again. I rubbed the folded pages' creases and put it on my bed and headed to the kitchen. It was late evening, and as soon as I opened the dining room door, Diana's voice, heavy as if weighed by night and loaded with melancholy, emanated from the darkness. I jolted back. Is that you, Hannah? I turned the light on. Yes, I said, still standing by the door. Jazz played from a stereo behind her. The kitchen smelt of whisky. There was a bottle of whisky and another of red wine in front of her. What're you doing here at this time? I asked. I'm here every night, she said. Don't ask me why. I want to get water, I said. She switched on a table lamp behind her, and the light engulfed her sadness with golden streaks. Diana, are you OK? She responded with a question: Did you enjoy your walk earlier? I didn't go out far, I said. Don't you worry about it, Diana said, and reassured me that the Home Office would send me their decision in no time. How do you know? Diana snorted: I'm bad at many things, but I still have faith in my gut instinct, she said. Thank you, I said. I'll be heading back to my room. Hannah? Yes. Do you sleep well? I wanted to respond when she interrupted me. I shouldn't have asked that, she said. I mean, it's a silly question. I mean, it's difficult for you, isn't it? You know, being new here. Diana, I'm alright, I said. But she continued: I'm sorry about what this country's putting you through when they know well you've suffered enough already. Her breath wafted towards me. Did you eat fish? I asked her. She laughed. No, she said. I happen to have kissed a fishmonger earlier. Her laughter vanished. She was still in the green long-sleeved V-neck dress she had worn for her night out. How was your meeting with your friend? I asked her. Date, she said, correcting me. It was a date. She sniggered. Sort of OK, she said. It's my fate. I'll forever keep looking for love like those searching for a home. Silence. Diana groaned: Oh, God, I'm sorry, Hannah. Don't be, I said. Love and a safe country both need finding and might never be found. Diana rushed around the table and hugged me. And I remembered the following morning, as I stood naked by my window watching the sunrise, how her breasts pressed against mine. Her chest was like a room full of secrets. I remember vowing not to add to her problems and to keep my issues to myself. I learnt a few songs from *Top of the Pops*, which I wrote out with the help of Diana. One evening, when Diana was in the living room watching the news, I made tea, singing, *I wanted to hear / Spinnin' mi round like a wheel on fire / Walkin'... on tightrope, my love's high wire...* I was on the way to my room with my cuppa when Anne, in a sleeveless black glittering long dress with side slits, hurled past me on her way down. I stumbled. Tea spilt on my trousers. I shrieked. She hissed: Can you not see? But you fucking refugees have no spatial awareness, do you? How about you? I said. You're not from here. She chortled. I came here like the Queen I am, said Anne, who was adopted as a young girl. I was a chosen one, unlike you, bitch, selling your story to the Home Office. Oh, please believe my story, please accept me. My hand shook as I firmed my grip around the handle of my cup, about to throw the tea at her saggy breasts popping out through her dress's low neckline. What are you going to do? Go on, she said. When she stepped closer, her face touching mine, the darkness in her eyes aroused me. Warmth invaded me with each of her breaths. She put an arm around my neck and held my chin with her fingers: Ooh baby, don't be sad now, she said. Go upstairs and do whatever you do up there. I have serious fucking to do. I ran to my room and shut the door. I placed my cup on my desk and threw myself into bed. I was wet between my legs, though I doubted the tea had touched my skin. What touched me was lust. My mind tried to make sense of what had happened. The feeling was as unfamiliar as this new country. It was as if the seas I had crossed to get here had washed my insides, softened the borders within me so that my shame, guilt, pleasure and pain all jumbled up, exchanging places and meanings. I came as a refugee seeking a safe place, a home where I could achieve my family's dreams, but in those lonely days and nights at Diana's it was my desires that flourished. The throbbing on my thighs burnt and excited me at the same time. Pain was the ignition of my pleasure: it scorched the doubts that formed in my mind about the purpose of my being. A throaty voice somewhere inside me – and I can't remember when or why I had labelled the voices I held inside me as a way of distinguishing between them, as if to give the multitude of my identity a voice – rose from a long slumber, ready to hurl accusations of selfishness at me. But that voice of reason soon incinerated between my thighs, pulsating, pumping out a sensation. I opened the window and invited the London night into my room. And London arrived carrying conversations of people on the verge of being born, dying, creating, singing, seducing, of killing and being killed, speaking in hundreds of different languages, and of Anne about to fuck someone somewhere. I had yet to discover London in all its dimensions, in the way it discovered me in my room, because at that moment, and though I had been at Diana's house for some time, I hadn't ventured out as much as I should have. Jazz blew into my room with the songs of a city that fragmented itself among its citizens. I opened my body, my soul, my mind to London when I stood naked by my window, when I cried by my window, when I masturbated standing by my window, when I thought silly thoughts and others that were as profound as the ones I encountered in the books I read by the window. I combed my hair as my eyes chased the Jubilee trains. I massaged the back of my neck as I ogled a sky beading melancholy in its clouds. I sat on a chair by the window and raised my legs, so that the lips of my thighs would be the source of the wind swirling around Londoners' nostrils. The morning found me awake. The sun seeped through my window and my eyelids. As if determined to cement my relationship with London, as strong as it was in my head, I followed Diana's advice and headed out for a stroll in my neighbourhood. The window of the building opposite Diana's house was open. I glowered at the curtains, which drifted in and out with the breeze. The presence of his silhouette weighed heavier in the silence. I returned to my room, to the rush-hour trains storming one after another through the mist that rose over the rail tracks, ferrying passengers to work, schools, places of dance, acting and decision-making, to visit families. Yet I had to sit out another day in my room. Bitterness fed on the emptiness of every day I spent waiting for a decision on my application. Suspicions seeded in my mind: this was designed so that those of us who came to this country with high hopes would be stripped of our aspirations slowly, emptied of our determination, and we would learn to let go of our goals and, in time, come to terms with the fact that our function in this country was to act as a ladder to British people's success. This belief grew when Diana told me that like Anne, Bina-Balozi also worked in a fast-food restaurant. I surrendered to mistrust. I imagined the Home Office officers, those tasked with determining the credibility of my story, were on the Jubilee line, peering at me as if waiting to witness the flight of my sanity out through my window. I drew the curtains and sat in my bed in a morning darkened by fear, and fear like a black hole sucked the light out of my mind. At moments like this, my room in London resembled a prison island within the British Isles. I remember sitting on the floor, my arms around my knees, I remember imagining being deported but not having any reaction to it, I remember thinking about my childhood sweetheart, Alem, and the times we showered together, I remember lying on the sofa reading more of Diana's books and entering debates with characters and writers as if I were the centre of the dinner parties taking place on the pages, I remember talking to Diana about literature and her suggesting writers I might like. There's more BB. I remember one day, I watched a man on TV and liked something about him but wasn't sure what it was, and it was in my sleep I discovered how he made my heart leap. Darkness revealed the glow of my desires. I remember more and more fantasies coming into my head on those sleepless nights, I remember fearing that my head would overflow with them, I remember

I was telling myself that I didn't want to hide those fantasies like my father had hidden his books in the ground but that I wanted to show them in the way that Diana displayed her books, when I heard a thud. I thought it was the Jubilee line, but the rail tracks had long shut down for the night. The bang grew louder. I opened my door. It was Anne. She stood in her robe, barefoot. Hello slacker, she said. I'm not, I said. You are, she said, sitting here waiting for me to feed you. You don't, I said. I pay the taxes for your lazy ass to lie in that bed all day long. Come, I have a job for you, she said. I can't work, I said. The lawyer told me I wasn't allowed to. She cackled. Oh Lord, you thick everywhere, ha. Your job title is ass cleaner, she said, chuckling. I'm on my way to get laid and I want you to make sure it's clean. I made to shut my door, but she held it. It was a joke, she said. Honestly. Well, maybe you need to work on your jokes, I said. She simpered. Good comeback, she said, adding, Listen, can you help me get a bottle of shampoo from the top shelf? I hadn't realised she was this short, and she didn't wear high heels to compensate. My craving for her had elevated her stature above mine, and her confidence had lengthened her presence in my mind beyond her actual size. I thought about desire and how it exaggerates our impressions of those we long for. In the morning, I ran downstairs. Diana asked me to join her for breakfast. I declined, and I was about to leave with a banana when the front door opened. It must be my darling, Diana said, springing to her feet. I didn't know that he still had the keys to the house. She rushed to meet him. Bina- Balozi entered the dining room, holding flowers. Isn't he lovely? Diana said as she introduced him to me. She took the bouquet from his hand and pranced to the kitchen to get a vase. When he extended his hand to shake mine, I examined his hand and his long pinkie nail. A mere sighting of his skin set me off to roam beyond the confinement of my world in that room. I gasped at the speed with which I fantasised about him, but the feelings filtered deeper, and our encounter on the bench of Fitzroy Square had its roots in that morning when I saw him for the first time in Diana's house in Kilburn. It was a beautiful morning, or it was the discovery of the bestial and assertive version of myself at the first presence of BB that turned it into a memorable morning. Diana called Anne to come and see Bina-Balozi. Anne appeared in her bathrobe. She had her hair in a bun. She slapped Bina-Balozi's backside: Alright, brother? Hey, Anne, my beautiful sis. They hugged. Anne, thank you for lending me the money the other day, he said. I'll give it to you at the end of the month. Don't worry about it, brother, but I need my thong back, Anne said. What thong? asked Diana, now back with a blue glass vase that she placed on the dining room table next to the fruit bowl. Nothing to worry about, Bina-Balozi said. Well, duh, said Anne. This perv took my thong because this girl he's into likes them on her boys. What the fuck is this world coming to? Sis, shut it now, Bina-Balozi said. You're embarrassing me in front of this new girl here. Whatever, perv, said Anne. Bina-Balozi brought his hand to his face and chortled. My giggle drew his attention. What's your name again? he asked me. Refugee, Anne answered on my behalf. Anne, enough, said Diana. D, a bit of banter won't hurt her. This is London she fled to, right, Bina-Balozi? Definitely, Bina-Balozi said. You won't survive London without a sense of humour. If you don't like jokes, you become the joke around here. Like they say, fun is the name of the game. I'll be back, Diana said, and dashed to the

toilet upstairs. Anne stepped towards me: Have you heard
that? Fun is the name of the game in London. My heart
palpitated at her morning breath. What, are you going to
sob now? Go on. I could use your tears to soothe myself.
I tell ya, that was a serious double-dicks I had yesterday.
I bet your Somali back would've broken into pieces. I'm not
Somali, I said. Y'all look the same, hun. You're one of us, I
wanted to tell her, but when she kissed her teeth it was as if
she sucked the air out of me. She turned around, picked an
apple from the bowl and took a bite. Sheeet, she said. This
shit is sour as hell. Her face twisted into a grimace. Anyway,
we move, said Anne. She took another mouthful of the
apple and asked Bina-Balozi if he wanted a bite. He shook
his head. I'm OK, sis. Brother, you're losing weight. Are you
not eating or what? I am, said Bina-Balozi, but my worries
are like worms, sis. You know you can talk to me anytime
you want, Anne said. I'm here for you. The two stood by the
door and Bina-Balozi slipped his hands into the pockets of
his jacket. Anne leant against the wall and crossed one leg
over the other. My ears dwelt on their accents, which fluc-
tuated between the type I had heard on the evening news,
that of the man by the window, and something I had caught
the few times I had been out on Kilburn High Road. The
way they spoke combined nasal irony, emotional expressions,
melancholy, wounds that leapt to my ears with sorrowful
exuberance. I longed to mimic the way they let *English*
lounge at the tip of their tongues – a language that became
serious, playful, hesitant and rich in foreign syntax as it
churned on their life experiences before it was spoken.
I put the banana back in the bowl. Anne untied her bun and
let her hair fall to its full length, hanging over her shoulders.
So, what are you up to these days? asked Anne. Work, sis,

that's all. I'm working three shifts. I want to build my mother a new house back home. That's my priority now. Hang in there, brother, Anne said. And after a moment of silence, she added: I wish I had a family back in the motherland to treat like this. But at the same time, knowing me, I can't deal with expectations. She laughed. But Bina-Balozi pulled her towards him. Come here, sis, he said. After a long embrace, Anne peeled herself away. Anyway, brother, I'm heading back to my room, but I'll take you out for yummy Italian food soonish. I know you love pizza. Blessed to have you in my life, sis, said Bina-Balozi. Anne fetched coffee from the breakfast table and left. Bina-Balozi and I were alone. He took his eyes off me and tapped his foot as he glanced around. I stared at him and then at the blue vase, as if I could see his reflection in the assortment of roses he'd brought for Diana. As if flowers, as I believed, were the mirror for a person's interior, I lowered my head to ponder what I perceived to have seen of Bina-Balozi's inside, when I spotted my fly was wide open. I was commando, and my pubic hair poked through. Are you two still standing? Diana asked, back from the toilet. Why don't you take a seat while I put the kettle on? She asked me to join her and Bina-B. I was going to turn down her invitation and return to my room when Bina-Balozi took off his jacket, and I noticed his bottom as he turned around to drape his jacket over the chair. I stood still. He pulled up his trousers over his thighs. The sight of his perky and round bum triggered my brain. I felt a bull charging through my blood to mount his rear. Baffled and breathless, I wiped my sweat. Hannah? Yes, Diana. Are you OK, sweetheart. Yes, I said. I am. I gulped for air. I'll make the tea, I said. In the kitchen, my mind wandered back to Bina-Balozi. His bottom had set off my imagination.

The forces of my desires talked to me – they blew thoughts like lava, as if, in my mind, we could only make love when we had become specks of ashes scattered in the wind, beyond recognition in form or shape. I paced up and down, lost, until I was snapped back from my world by the kettle's whistle. I brought the tea to the dining room table with a plate of biscuits. I sat and observed Bina-Balozi as he listened to Diana without interruption. Thoughts fermented in my mind during his long silence, and I held on to many of them long after he'd left and I'd returned to my room. The mere sight of him brought up so many questions. How could I have feelings about him and Anne, two different people, at the same time, with the same intensity? My room turned into a laboratory where I experimented with my desires. In the absence of a Home Office decision, of school, education or family, sex loomed large in my life, and everything else faded into the night. If my passion for men's asses is a condition I suffer from, then it must be called reciprocity: the need to enter and see inside my male lover in the way they could. I yearned for every part of their body to be accessible to the variations of my desires in the way I was to them. But it could also be a mere addiction to an anus that I first discovered when I was with Alem in that open-roofed shower, when I washed his body and took the dust off his skin to reveal a gateway between his cheeks that was more than a hole – that the more I pressed with my tongue through his *O*, the more it added intricacy to my palates. In those days, while waiting for the Home Office to decide on my application, and while living in a room bordered by a train line on one side and the man in the first-floor window on the other, every dark tunnel had the promise of light at its end. O Bina-B. I remember that moment in Fitzroy Square after I had finished topping him and said to him, Fuck me now. The weather oscillated between wet and warm, windy and calm. But my obsession was the weather I was creating inside Bina-B. As I glimpsed the lush spring I had brought to his body in that rainy night, I thought that if I could reinvent weather, I could also reinvent love. The lights drifted on the backs of poets' silhouettes strolling on the deserted streets of Fitzroy Square in the way BB floated around my heart. I don't remember if I or Bina-B had said it, but one of us muttered: *There's a certain kind of loneliness to falling in love.* O. B.B. I want you to fuck me now. As soon as these words left my lips, he bowed his head. When even the idea of fucking me, which many had taken for granted, made him hesitate, satisfaction invaded me. That was the world I wanted to be part of, a world where reciprocity is the key to pleasure, a world where the certainty we were born into is replaced by one constantly altering according to our changing feelings and ideas, a world where the only certitude is to experience freely as we go along. BB held my hand. Our bodies glued, our eyes locked. It was as if he'd pinned me against the raging sky: lightning flashed through my skin, and as I trembled, I hunted the black panthers in his eyes. A rainbow appeared in the clouds of his breath. He parted my legs. There was no pushing, no thrusting. He arrived inside me like a sensitive visitor who takes off their shoes and all their expectations and leaves them by the door. Once he was inside me, he didn't move. His mouth was as silent as his penis. He leant towards me. On our breaths sailed out the history of violence, wars against the colonisers, civil wars, the alien religions, the definitions, the traumas and migrations. Silence moved in our veins, floating under our pores as if we had smuggled our Nile to this spring night, fertilising our imaginations. The weight was in his chest, filled with stories that he pressed against mine. I never felt anything deeper as he made love to me with the words of a folklore story he recited about humans in the shape of trees hanging from the skyline. Bina-Balozi was what you call a child soldier, although his fights were not to free a country, but himself. He was four when his father carried him on his shoulders to the market of their village. Bina-Balozi lowered his head towards his father that day and said, Daddy, I want to be like my mother when I grow up. The father pulled his son down and smacked him. But this only increased Bina-Balozi's determination. He watched his mother as she worked various jobs in the village and at home, while his father drank and gambled her money away. Bina-Balozi copied her in every single way possible: how she wended through the narrow streets of her village and life, how she listened to the silence around her, how she smiled, laughed and cooked, and how her face twitched and itched. The way she walked, throwing her hips about, found its way to my lap. Oh, Bina-B. When Bina-Balozi turned nine, people noticed the similarities between him and his mother. He was as tall and thin as her. A time came when teenage Bina-Balozi turned himself into an identical twin of his mother, as he had always wanted. From Bina-Balozi, I sharpened my belief that we can rebirth ourselves if we have an imagination. Imaginations are genderless wombs. Bina-Balozi's life in his hometown ended one night after his father returned home drunk and entered the tin hut the family of three shared, holding his torch. The father shook his sleeping wife and asked her to get up because He Was Hungry. Bina-Balozi saw everything and knew what kind of hunger the father had in mind. I'm going to urinate, and when I come back, I want you ready, the father said to his wife, stuttering out of the tin hut surrounded by trees. Bina-Balozi followed his father and waited for him outside. The father pissed against a tree, and when he turned, he flashed his torch light on Bina-Balozi, now wearing his mother's dress. Amma, what are you doing here? the father asked Bina-Balozi. Let's do it there, Bina-Balozi said in his mother's voice that became his. Holding his father's hand, he walked him away from the hut. The father was never seen again. Bina-Balozi left for London. Peace and prosperity came to his mother from the future she'd sown in her son. Bina-Balozi built her a new cement house and continued to send her half of his monthly income. O Bina-B. That same afternoon I saw Bina-B at Diana's house for the first time and as he aroused variations of power and dynamism inside me, Diana and I devoured the dish of meat stew with potatoes we had cooked. I spent the rest of that day in my room staring at my mother's diary in my hand. Whenever I opened a page, my mind raced through the scenarios I feared encountering next. Her first entry had set the scene that something strange had happened between her and my father. This was to be my programme for the weeks that followed. Whenever Diana suggested we take a long walk to discover other parts of London, I wavered between accepting her proposition and staying indoors. Other than the man living in the opposite building, I also feared loving London too much when not certain if the Home Office would allow me to stay. When I shared this with Diana, she told me that she had the same fear of men. And all types of fear limit relationships, she said. One morning, I woke up thinking about her words and put on my clothes and exited the house for a stroll without washing my face. The sleep in my eyes veiled my view. I wiped off the mucus and raised my head. Looking up at the opposite window after leaving the house became as mandatory as checking for cars before crossing a street. The man had a grey suit on, and his tie dangled as he leant through the window to light a cigarette. He took a long drag and blew out the smoke in circles that clouded my mind. For a moment, I thought he was the man dealing with my case at the Home Office. The confidence with which he yelled, Our country, our city, our street, convinced me that no matter how well I spoke English and integrated into this society, I would never be as British as him. That was when I thought it would be easier to love this city and this country from a distance, from my room. I returned to my room and my inner world. Looking back, I can see that it was in that confined room in Kilburn, trapped between that man at the window and the rail track, that I became the person who clasped Bina-B's waist on that bench in Fitzroy Square: a creature made of melancholy, a bull with wings and horns made of ideas. I remember one morning, as I stood by the window and bathed in London's sunrise, following the Jubilee line trains in their rush hour, thinking of Bina-Balozi's body, as radiant as when I'd first seen him days earlier, I remember trying to supress my desires, I remember how this urge to restrain my mind aroused another voice that urged me to let go. Competing voices filled my head. I remember thinking about the peanut butter on sliced white bread with bananas and a bit of honey that Diana had made for me and which I ate as I watched *Top of the Pops*, I remember thinking there was a difference between the English written in books and that in songs, I remember stealing fashion tips from a singer

performing half-naked on the stage and walking around
my room in a new pair of boxer shorts and a red plaid shirt
I'd purchased at a men's shop with Diana, I remember
the male singers in make-up – from those with eyeliner
to those who daubed their faces with designs to free the
satanic and angelic spirits within them – and taking some
of them out for a date in a quiet corner of my head. O BB.
I remember thinking the stage was the freest place in
England, and dreaming of becoming a singer, I remember
having my first ever coffee, which sent me on a mental trip
so powerful that I've wanted to substitute coffee for English
tea ever since, but Diana insisted I shouldn't. Was it because
Diana suspected I had an addictive personality? I remember
listening to Diana a lot during those days, like that evening
she convinced me that I was the future of this country,
I remember being confused and asking her for clarification.
Do you mean Eritrea? I meant the UK, she said, but I'm sure
you're the future of Eritrea too. The future of the UK? I asked
again. This country that doesn't recognise me yet. Yes, she
said. Yes. I bought into her optimism that evening, as I
closed the door behind me and my head opened to a breeze
chiming with a future as lush as the Yorkshire field Diana
talked about, when I heard his voice. I was about to turn
back, but I remembered what Diana had told me, and I
enacted the script. Accept it, I said to him. I'm this country's
future. He snorted. You don't even speak English. Maybe
not like you, but I do, I said. And you don't need to speak
to love someone or something anyway. Fuck off, he said,
throwing words heavy as stones. Refugee. Sicko. Diana came
out in her pyjamas. Police were called. They would investigate
him, they promised. But they had been promising Diana
such investigations for years. I shut myself in my room and

continued to visit London through my window, listening to its greed for life through the Jubilee line that marched along to 'Saturday Night Fever' playing on my radio. Diana urged me to resist isolation. This is your London, she said again and again. You need to push through it all, she told me one morning as she pleaded with me to go grocery shopping with her. And we were out on Kilburn High Road one evening when a mixed aroma wafted from London's skin, as if its pores were composed of people from everywhere. But if you asked me how London smelt in those early weeks, I would say not of curry, or Eritrean stew, or fish and chips, or this and that, but of rain, how the downpour washed the varieties of its inhabitants and their breaths to a lake that rested between Anne's legs. I found her scent in a pair of underwear that, like a cradle, held her stains. Anne was a distraction, and I became her distraction too, but from what? I would not know, though I would keep trying to figure it out. O. BB, curiosity is the fuel of my desire, I said as I parted the cheeks of his bottom. O.B.B. I met Anne in my dreams more often than in real life, and she became so blurred in my vision that I didn't know what attracted me most – the real Anne or the version of her I had created in my imagination. As time passed, with me locked inside Diana's house, my mind took such a flight from reality that I was convinced I lived in an abstract world. I could see what I longed for but couldn't touch it, like the peace I had left my country for, believing it was guaranteed on arrival at my destination. In my room in Kilburn, I didn't hear bombs at night but I lived with the deafening sound of the voices in my head rising to converse with each other. One morning, I found Diana in the kitchen with a bag that, she told me, Anne had left by her door the night before with a note: *For you to wear for your new date. Love ya.* She made further contributions to Diana's home, like changing the fridge. But I didn't dwell on what Anne did. Her tenderness was peripheral. I needed the empathy of her dark side in that phase of my life. I craved to be the forest for the black panther that roamed inside her. I waited for her – she was bound to be hungry one day. The other thing of significance that happened during that time was that whenever I scurried to the kitchen in the middle of the night, I found Diana with her bottle of wine, surrounded by smoke. She only smoked by night, as if she sought the invisibility the darkness brought along with it. One night, after reading a few pages from my mother's diary, I headed downstairs. I cannot say whether my mother's diary, and the frankness with which she wrote about her sex life in the middle of a war zone, informed my sexual choices and led me to that bench in Fitzroy Square, ogling the moist cracks of Bina-B's cheeks. Are we susceptible to what we read, especially if the words are the only confirmation we have of the presence of those we love but who are gone? *Monday. 3.30 a.m.: It's been a few days since that night Xehay told me he couldn't have sex. All I've been doing is thinking about him and what he said. I can't imagine a life without sex. But can't imagine a life without him. Then again, I feel that the absence of intercourse will only challenge us to voyage to the extreme to find the same thrills other couples find through penetration. I'll guide us to get there, although I have to say that for someone who can't read and write, Xehay is highly literate in the anatomy of his desires. He knows what he wants. Last night, he held my foot and stared at it for hours as I did my reading. He only interrupted me when he asked for the frankincense gum I was chewing. After he chewed it for a bit, he said he'd extracted all my mouth juice from the gum.*

I poured more of my saliva into his mouth. I still marvel at moments like this, when the universe brings things I thought were mere fantasies into my lap. I was caught between a moment of belief and disbelief. I had to pinch him, strike him, and hear his screams to know he was real. Diana sat surrounded by her thoughts, as thick as the clouds of smoke. I glided past her and stared at her silhouette on the wall behind, steady as a portrait. The clouds pouring out of her chest followed me to my room. I sat by my window, and my mind stretched between the man across the road, the Home Office in Surrey, my past and family in Eritrea, Anne, BB, Diana. Contrasting thoughts, contradictory feelings and many weighty opposites pulled my mind here and there, so much that I snapped one night. I sprinted outside the house barefoot and in my pyjamas and ran up and down the street. And on another night, on the back of many sleepless nights, with the rain sounding like the bullets I grew up with back home and the clouds of London mushrooming like the clouds of dust that rose in my hometown after bombardment, I opened the window and sat on the ledge. *Everything passes, love remains –* ኩሉ ይሓልፍ ፍቅሪ ትቐጽል *– kullu yihalif, fiqri yiterif.* An explosion set off in the distance. The fireworks scattered in London's sky, painting colours and shapes against the night so spectacular that they brought a smile to my face. I returned to my bed and slipped under my blanket. I remember waking up the next morning with nothing on my mind, I remember deciding to watch TV all day long, I remember the breakfast programme that left me wondering if this country was the right country for me, but then changed my mind when the presenter laughed and I chortled along, I remember the guest who spoke about his desire to get England fit again, I remember standing to stretch and move to the tune of the music blasting behind him, I remember the weatherman whose face looked like a funeral as he stated the prediction for the day ahead, I remember asking Diana about it, and in response her telling me that since that weatherman who had denied a hurricane was on the way a few years earlier, all weather presenters had become sombre when reporting on pending storms, I remember her laughing and saying, OK, I might be exaggerating, I remember teasing her about the misinformation and returning to watching TV, I remember a late afternoon show where old women sat in a circle talking. They all had thick feet and ankles, which I asked Diana about. I remember her telling me that she thought what they had was called edema, I remember looking for it in the dictionary, from which I drank some words and weird English idioms such as *all mouth and no trousers* and *donkey's years*, I remember dancing along in front of the TV while watching a show about ballroom dancing, I remember laughing when Diana told me she was going to the toilet, saying, It's a number two, I remember Diana calling me once from the dining room to tell me Anne had called to say she'd buy us a new cooker, I remember whenever I asked her about Anne's whereabouts she'd tell me, I don't know, or I can't say much. But she was happy to talk about Bina-Balozi. I remember her telling me about him one late afternoon while she cooked pasta with tomato sauce as I ironed clothes. On that rainy evening in Fitzroy Square, steam poured out of Bina-B's mouth. He was as hot as a charcoal iron whose cavity was filled with smouldering coals. I wanted to hold him, to thaw the cold in my chest, but Bina-B shuffled his feet and slid backwards towards the flowers behind him, which wilted under the weight of the rain in the gated gardens of Fitzroy Square.

O Bina-B. O. B.B. But in my room in Kilburn, my fantasy of Bina-Balozi nestled like a beauty spot between my breasts. The last train of the day released cool into the air, and tranquillity trickled through my window. I opened my mother's diary and stared at it without reading. I put it aside and left for the kitchen. But that night, instead of fetching a glass of water, I pulled up a chair and sat opposite Diana. She fanned the smoke away, but her face took a while to emerge from its clouds. The biggest veil for those who want to hide comes from within, I thought. Diana was on my mind when I looked into BB's eyes on Fitzroy Square and thought: some of us don't strive to find our true selves because we long to remain mysterious. I was thinking of shadows and fragments when I remembered the refined version of Diana in the mornings as she did her paperwork and looked after us. A quest for the self is a quest for a reflection of what we yearn to be in a particular moment. I knew that because my quests were as numerous as my desires, which varied with my moods and were triggered by contrasting feelings. I thought Diana donned a mask to give us a welcoming experience at her house, as she was also bound by her agreement with the refugee organisation. But on encountering her in the kitchen that night, I wanted to ask her to always be herself, and I had this urge to offer her a home in me in the way she sheltered me with all my history, fears and dreams. I hadn't thought about this kind of exile before, one where people migrate with their feelings to those nearest and dearest to them. Diana placed a hand on mine and asked if I was OK. I am, I said. I just want to join you in your silence. Of course, sweetheart, she said, and sipped on her wine as she scanned the magazine in front of her. How she could see in the dull light reminded me of my blind relative who told us she could read our interiors. Words, too, had a galaxy of stars floating under their skins. Diana drank half her glass of wine. I thought once again how similar we looked. We were twins separated by seas, languages, religions and nationalities. Diana switched on the table lamp in the corner of the dining room. I looked at her shadow on the wall and took fragments of her back to my room. I sat in bed to read my mother's diary. *Friday. 3.30 a.m.: I was angry earlier today. According to my friends, I'm miserable. But maybe I have a different idea of happiness. Another contentious moment with my friends occurred when I told them about Xehay. In their eyes, he's a pathetic coward. They urged me to find a stronger man. I understand why they saw Xehay as weak for surrendering to me, because they submit to their men. They retorted when I reminded them of that, saying I was trying to be like the Italians. I got upset and told them the history of matriarchal African societies dismantled by foreign invaders. I often have to use stories from our past to validate how I want to live my present. Anyway, Xehay's the bravest man I know, because he fights for the type of love he wants, for what brings him pleasure. And I'll protect him. Oh, I still remember those early days with Xehay. When I grasped his untapped passion was vital to anchoring him to my world. I opened his body to me and made him see his skin was full of treasures that I would excavate with my nails, teeth and wrath. Yesterday, I tied him to my bed and drew shapes of flowers all over his skin. He was a garden with wilting daisies. I stood over him and showered him with the rain of my womb.* Another day passed, and the relationship between my parents continued to occupy my mind for some time to come. But I couldn't get rid of the diary. It was my history. Do we choose history? Can we select a less disturbing part while throwing the rest away? My head was filled with questions as I joined Diana in the dining room another night. She sat next to a pile of letters and opened envelopes with jagged edges. The jazz on the stereo was upbeat. She tossed her hair to the side and turned a page of her magazine. Later, a moment of mirth interrupted our silence when Diana read out loud a letter from the agony aunt column, in which the writer sought advice about her husband of ten years who no longer wanted to have sex but whom she was still drawn to. In her response, the agony aunt talked about therapy, but I made Diana laugh when I said: Why doesn't the woman fuck her husband? I took that question I blurted out to Diana to my bed and into my dream. One morning, I woke up feeling eighteen. I was sure I had turned eighteen some time ago but didn't want to believe that it found me still in my room, still stateless and without school. Diana was in the living room speaking to her aunt, who lived in an elderly care home. I sat on the sofa with a book from Diana's shelf on African American history. She was about to hang up when her eighty-one-year-old aunt asked to speak to me. I took the handset after a moment of hesitation, and Diana caressed my back as she whispered that her aunt was lovely. But she didn't tell me she was funny too. The aunt told me something about Diana that stayed with me: Diana had left her parents' home in Yorkshire for London when she was sixteen to pursue her dreams. Diana will tell you the rest, the aunt said, making me promise to come and see her with Diana in York, but she added: Hopefully I'll still be around. She corrected my assumption when I wished her a long life: Oh, my dear, I don't plan to die anytime soon, she said. She had fallen in love with a man at the care home who was due to move to Devon: And, she said, I'm thinking of going with him. But don't tell Diana any of this yet. I promised I wouldn't, and before I hung up she said, Welcome home. The UK is your country now. I didn't need to wait for the Home Office to approve my application, she told me. The UK is my home, I repeated every morning for the next few days, as I scuttled downstairs whenever the letterbox rattled. Most letters were addressed to Diana, and a few to Anne. Some of the letters to Diana had the word URGENT in red capital letters on top of the envelopes. I thought about what might have been urgent in her life, as I headed back to my room and waited for the next delivery. In my bed, I thought about Bina-Balozi and Anne. I remember that evening when it was dark inside me, when another day passed without a decision on my case, when I took my sadness downstairs to the dining room where Diana sat and inhaled her smoke. The jazz singer on the stereo sang that spring was in the air, but I shivered in the winter of the dining room. Diana hunched until her breasts touched her stomach and her back could fold no more. I remembered what her auntie told me over the phone about Diana leaving home when she turned sixteen: My dear, there's something sentimental about those who chase something when young. And I also remembered Diana telling me she had trained as a social worker in her early forties. That was when I asked: Diana, what did you study at university? She snorted and then fell silent. I waited for her to speak. Nothing. I'm sorry I asked, I said after a while. No, no, Hannah. It's not that. You reminded me... Well, let me think... She paused. Again, I waited for her to resume her sentence, but she drifted into a long silence. She blinked and then closed her eyes. It was as if she had stored her memories outside herself, in a tin she had kicked down a hill to an irretrievable place. Recalling how my father suffered whenever he reminisced about his time with my mother, I thought Diana and he shared common traits. I now wonder if some choose to live in their memories for masochistic reasons. *Everything passes, love remains – kullu yihalif, fiqri yiterif –* ኩሉ ይሓልፍ ፍቕሪ ትቕጽል. An excerpt from my mother's diary I had read earlier was on my mind as I headed to the kitchen to make tea with cardamom and cloves on the new cooker Anne had bought for Diana. *Saturday. 2 a.m.: My father speaks English to me, my mother Italian, our helper Tigrinya, and my teachers Amharic. But Xehay and I talk in a language that is not written and can't be read, and is enriched and deepened with our love. So, we make love all the time. Yesterday morning, I invited him to my room for a quick one before I headed to my college. We giggled as I smeared his neck with my orgasms and left.* I returned to my seat opposite Diana. Mm, smells nice, Diana said. I don't remember if it was that same night or another, but I persisted with the question: Diana, are you happy with what you studied? She snickered: Being happy with your studies, I discovered to my cost, is a false dawn. I was a good student and achieved great results, but all that would mean nothing in a society that... She paused and was again about to fall back into silence. This time, I tried to keep the conversation going. What did you want to say about society, Diana? It's nothing, sweetheart. It must be something, I said. Otherwise you'd have told me. Listen, sweetheart, she said. I did a BA in drama and art in London, but I gave up my dream and retrained as a social worker soon after. Well, not soon after, but years after being unemployed, trying a few things and going nowhere with my degree. They say art is a luxury, and they're right, maybe more so for people like us. Anyway, I'm happy doing something meaningful now. She fell silent. I grabbed her glass and took a gulp. Let's go for a walk, Diana. It's late, sweetheart, she said. I stood up. Please, D. It will do us good, innit? Diana laughed. You're learning fast from Anne, she said. I wish I could see her more, I said. She'll be back, Diana said. I used to be like her. Sometimes we need to disappear to come back more rounded. She put on her jacket. I pulled the bundle of her hair from underneath her scarf, adjusting it on the dark blue suede collar. She buttoned her jacket and indicated with her arm, Let's Go, Baby, when she said she needed to use the bathroom. I'll wait outside, I said. The air blew through my curls. As if I longed to be touched, as if nature was a reincarnation of my father, I crossed my arms and leant against the wind. My face glinted in the light of my thoughts like lanterns dotted around my head. I yearned for this embrace to tighten, for this moment to go on, but the man's voice boomed through the deserted street, and my bones. Oi, you. I didn't look up. I doubted myself, as if I hadn't left this spot since he had hurled obscenities at me days before, since the first morning I arrived at Diana's house. This was his power. He held me captive to a moment, shackled me to a place. Diana came out of the house and pulled me by the arm. Ignore this asshole, she said. Go, he said to Diana, leaning his head further out of the window. But remember, you'll be responsible for a new plague. Diana raced across the street: Who the fuck are you calling rats? He slammed his window shut and turned the light off. Diana banged her fist on his door and planted her finger on his buzzer. Come out, you coward. I imagined him in his room, feet up, listening to the angry woman outside his building. I'm sorry, Diana. Please let's just go. But Diana kicked his door. I threw my arms around her. She was warm, as if her chest was an oven that burnt with the logs of racism, disappointment and misfortune. Please, Diana, let's go back home. No, Hannah, if I had to go home each time someone said something to me, I'd be locked in my house forever. Let's walk, she said. *Everything passes, love remains – kullu yihalif, fiqri yiterif –* ኩሉ ይሓልፍ ፍቅሪ ትቐጽል. Locking arms, Diana and I marched to Kilburn High Road. I listened to the sound of her heels on the stones. I thought about us, about the cultural differences I kept hearing on TV, and what they meant. We were born on different continents but looked the same. More than that, we had similar perspectives on many things – most of our culture came from books we read and writers we loved. We let each other be, and often we talked about how freedom within her house was as important as its existence outside. I often thought about the battles for her individual liberty in a colonised country that my mother narrated in her diary, and how much I tried to emulate her quest in London – to live as free as Diana, an Englishwoman, even though I had yet to be accepted as a refugee and allowed to live in this country. The absurdity of borders, nationalities magnified when Diana caressed my hand as we turned into the High Road and I felt the beating of her heart in my chest. I didn't need the Home Office's permission to be recognised, to see and feel Diana beyond those separations. We walked past a shop from where a man with a turban emerged with a child begging for sweets, and the man said, What you need my dear is sweet dreams, not candies. I laughed, so loud as to shake Diana out of her slumber. Her eyes surrendered to the silence of the dimly lit alley, where a man with a sleeping bag over his shoulders stroked a cat lying on a car's hood. Diana, are you OK? Her eyes were full of thoughts I couldn't decipher. I was about to look away when she said, I'll be OK. It's nothing

compared to what you've been through. I let go of her hand
and turned around. How strange: I thought of her sadness
in its own terms, not as a something put on a scale to weigh
against my own anguish. Hannah, what's up, sweetheart?
Everything passes, love remains – Kullu yihalif – ኩሉ ይሓልፍ.
We continued, and with every step I thought of my presence
in this country, which had now reached an impasse, and
how my love for this city grew on an idea of a future I could
only construct in my room, and in my head. This was the
point when I understood that I needed my fantasies. What
kept me alive were my desires, and the lust that slithered
through me as muddy and unpredictable as the Thames
I had yet to visit but saw on TV. A smile forced itself on me
when a cyclist rode his bike past us on one wheel whilst
pedalling, and I guffawed when a woman with white hair
waved at pedestrians through the window of a limousine
and gave us the finger. My father had long hair, I told Diana
as we ordered our drinks at a jazz bar. It was the blanket
for my dreams. In her diary, my mother wrote that she had
told him to grow it. Diana paid for her wine and my ginger
beer. Did she say why? she asked me as she fetched her
change. No, I said then, but I could've said what I had
imagined my mother's reasons were: that she liked to skim
her fingers through his hair, like the way she sailed through
life. And that smooth passage through life is something
I craved to inherit, this desire to glide through Bina-B's legs
to the well of peace inside him. O. B. B. There's a beauty in
fleeting moments, in temporality, in going through events
and moments in life without leaving traces except on the
skin of lovers – and BB understood this. Saxophone blasted
around us in that bar in Kilburn. I spotted a man in tight
jeans next to one of the glitter-lighted bottles scattered

around. Hannah, what are you smiling about? Diana asked me. I had a dream, I said, grinning. Oh, Hannah, dreams in bars are my favourite, she said. Sometimes, I go out with a book. When you're in a packed bar with a book, no one bothers you, because no one thinks you're alone. Diana rested her chin on her shoulder and looked at the floor. She was in her fifties, and I wondered about her friends. I often thought about them, but when she mentioned how she often visited bars and clubs alone with books, the thought occupied my mind. A man dressed in a white suit stepped onto the empty dance floor and mimicked a saxophone player. He turned and twisted, throwing his head back as he stared at the ceiling. Diana panted. Diana, is everything OK? I am, she said. I'll be fine, it's nothing to worry about. But I longed to talk about what troubled her. I asked: Diana, is it because you think I'm young that you don't want to tell me? Of course not, sweetheart, she said. But it was obvious to me now: she had my story in the file that the aid organisation passed on to her. She knew a lot about me, and I wasn't a mystery to her but a conduit for her sympathy. My story, which she found sad, as she told me on several occasions, was an obstacle in getting to know her the way she knew me. The way she used it as an excuse to shelter me from her past emphasised the weight of what I had experienced. A new song played, crowding out my thoughts. Diana, how do you dance to jazz? You don't, she said. You sit and let your soul dance. So we sat at a table at the far end of the bar and returned to silence. It was as if music had turned Diana's eyes into a dance floor for her memories. I looked deeper into them, and as her soul danced to the saxophone beats, I closed my eyes. In my head, I was squeezed between Bina-Balozi and Anne. This daydream stirred me and made me chuckle. Moments later, I was about to thank her for showing me how to dance to jazz when she admonished herself for her state. I'm sorry, Hannah. Don't be, I said, thinking how the music moved me too. She wrapped her hands around my wrists and took a deep breath. I'm better now, she said. I'm sure I heard her mumble a thank you as she sprang to the dance floor. But I didn't say anything to comfort her. It seemed my presence alone soothed her. I gasped at the power of my ability to heal others by the mere fact of carrying bigger traumas. I stormed out of the club. Diana followed me. Hannah, stop. What happened? We stood in the middle of the pavement. We were jostled by people who scolded and whistled at us as they passed around and between us. Yet the path between Diana and me was clearer. Life had been unkind to her, but I didn't come to this country to be a parable, an example or a comparison. I didn't take the long journey to be put in a museum for English people to come to remind themselves that life could be harder. This is not what I'm in this country for, I said. What are you talking about, Hannah? I stared at the double-decker night bus stopping ahead of us. I moved towards it, but Diana held me back. Hannah? My misgivings about the Home Office, about this country and Diana, deepened. Hannah, please talk to me. I opened my eyes to Diana's gaze probing me. Just then, something leapt to the fore of my mind: I was a prisoner in her house, unable to move on with my life as I waited for the Home Office's decision, yet I had a function. She needed me as much as I needed her. My anger thawed as if the realisation of a purpose, no matter how flawed, small, temporary, absurd, or built on misconstrued assumptions, strengthened my relationship with my life in those days. O. BB. I'm not sure, but I might have even smirked at this recognition of my value to her. Did I say anything to upset you? Diana asked me. No, you didn't, I said. I want to go home now. At home, the space between us shrank as we spent the night drinking. She wine, I English tea. We laughed, talked and shared memories. She told me about her visits to Jamaica and Ghana. I taught her words in Tigrinya, and I giggled as she repeated after me, *kemey*, *haftay*, *mar'ay*. One night, a Saturday that felt like every other day, Diana and I sat in the dining room, as usual, opposite each other. And, as usual, smoke coiled into the air. I grabbed her glass and took a sip. I swallowed the bitter taste, and after a few gulps a chill slid down my throat. And even though I don't recall the season of that night, I dressed to reflect the summer vibes. I imitated the singer who changed his style every time he appeared on TV, which made me wonder if his different-coloured eyes were also part of his search for different ways to present himself anew with every day. That night, I wore a shirt with one sleeve. I used the sleeve I had already removed from the seam with scissors as a neck scarf. I combined it with boxer shorts with mismatched socks. The green high heels I had on belonged to Diana. Her shoe size was smaller than mine, but I didn't mind having my toes squeezed, like I imagined being clasped between Anne and Bina-Balozi in bed. O Bina-B, give me your O. The thought of his bottom spreading in front of me had stroked my strap-on, which had siphoned all the lust from the wellspring of my desire. O. BB. It was as if I sank into the soaking-wet bench of Fitzroy Square. I couldn't see Bina-B anymore. But he confirmed his presence when he came closer and asked if I was OK. You've been quiet for a bit, he said. I told him that yes, I was, but that I needed silence now and then and he was welcome to leave if he couldn't handle that. I understand, he said. I'll wait. Take as long as you like, Hannah. O. B. B. Your presence is the silence I need, your *O* is the hole I crave to slip through to swim in the peace lapping against your ribcage. I don't know if I thought these things or if I said them out loud to BB, but back in Diana's dining room in Kilburn, she turned behind her and lowered the volume of the stereo on the table next to a pile of bills, packs of cigarettes and a comb. I skipped over to Diana and brushed her hair with the wide-toothed comb. She exhaled. When I pulled her hair to one side, it was as if the world tilted with her, and I imagined us in years to come living in such a universe that shifted shape to fit our out-of-place souls. I wrapped my arms around her. As if an oasis existed in my exiled body – and in my room, exile became as familiar to me as London was to a Londoner – I pulled her to my chest. We stayed like this for a moment. Then we said goodnight. I was tipsy as I made my way upstairs to my room. I paused by Anne's door. The black panther fixed its eyes on me, triggering my longing to wrestle with a beast. I knocked on the door, hoping for Anne to burst through it. No answer. I edged closer to the panther as if to dare myself to put my flesh at the tip of its jaws. I called Anne's name, and my desires echoed in the hallway. I took my hunger back to my room and stood by my window without clothes, watching the tracks murmuring as if the trill the trains left on the rails lingered long after they ceased operation. Plants on the sides of the tracks lengthened towards a moon that floated closer, as if piggybacking on the London clouds. I climbed through the window and sat on the ledge. I remembered my father dancing in our garden with my mother's picture, his silhouette floating on our flowers. Every memory, like a feather attached to my body, made wings that could fly me away from this stagnant present back to my past. My life, like my mind, hung on that ledge. I was in between societies and ideas, between the sexual energies inside me that stretched my desires towards Anne one day and Bina-B on another, between languages, between feeling safe and unsafe in a country that had once occupied mine and yet refused to open its doors fully to me. Then I heard a bang. It must be Anne, I thought. I peeled myself from the window and rushed to the corridor where the keeper of the beast stood next to her panther. The fragrance of lechery wafted from my flesh, covered in perspiration. Why are you naked? she asked. I didn't respond. Goodnight then, she said. Ah. Did she say goodnight to me? I couldn't remember a time when she'd spoken this softly to me. I staggered back to my bed. Perhaps this was the real Anne, and I had merely conceived a version of her that suited the fantasy I'd grown in my room. I needed to leave. I headed out for a walk. I held my breath as I opened and closed the front door behind me. There was one house window with the light switched on, and it was his. My room was a cell, and his house was a prison tower shining its searchlight. I planted my eyes on his window, expecting him to thrust his head out. He didn't show. I stood there, caught between fear and awe. The light streaming through his window caressed the deserted street with tenderness. I tiptoed to the main road. I turned my head around and jumped at the slightest noise. Terror colonised the sound of the night. I soldiered on. But when I noticed a man marching towards me from the other side, I ducked behind a bin on the pavement. Moments later, when I was under the bridge, I looked up. The pigeons' cooing receded to a murmur. On Kilburn High Road, I stood next to a twenty-four-hour convenience store. I was asked for a cigarette or lighter, which I didn't have, mistaken for a beggar, which I didn't mind, had change hurled at my feet, and was queried How much? the meaning of which I understood when the man asked me if I also did anal. A group emerged from a door to my left, line-dancing, going low, asking onlookers to join them. Kilburn was about to go low and groove when two men stormed out of a bar on the opposite side of the road and brawled. A shirtless man stopped before me. He sniffed and spat out a ball of phlegm. Give me your blazer, he said. No, I said. He came forward: That's a man's jacket anyway, he said, give it. I refused. Do you want me to stab you now? I'd rather you don't, I said. What the fuck? I'm not negotiating, he said, adding, darling. I'm not your darling, I said. I don't know you. Jesus, he said, and put his hand into his jeans pocket and took out a knife. *Everything passes, love remains – kullu yihalif, fiqri yiterif –* ኩሉ ይሓልፍ ፍቅሪ ትቅጽል. Back in my room without my jacket, I sat in bed with my mother's diary. That night, I didn't want to read. But as I held the leather-bound diary, I couldn't resist opening it. My mother's writing was small and scruffy, as if she had written in a hurry and had so much she wanted to say, and the urgency with which she wrote lured me to read: *Saturday. 4 a.m.: The older we become, the less playful we are. I never want to grow up. Last week in my college, our Eritrean teacher talked about our future in Amharic as enforced by the Ethiopian occupiers. I couldn't help thinking how sad he looked. Instead of listening to him, I closed my eyes and thought of Xehay. Earlier, I was having throbbing, cramping pains in my abdomen. I wanted pain relief. I asked Xehay to come to my room. I put candles on the large windowsill and followed him as he arrived at the gate and strode through our garden of lime, orange and hibiscus trees.*

I pushed my foot through the curtains, positioned it between the candles, and introduced my feet to Xehay's mouth. He was allowed into my room after licking my toes one by one. I instructed him to blindfold himself and to dance for me around the room cluttered with chairs, books, shoes and clothes. He stumbled here. I took off my dress. He fell against a chair. I stripped naked. Then I stood in his path. He crashed into me. We both fell to the floor with a thud. We have never laughed as hard. I love you, he said. I giggled as I kissed him, pulling at his lip with my teeth. I sat on his face, his bleeding mouth meeting my bleeding vagina. I ran to the bathroom and vomited. But was it possible to forget words already consumed? I screamed Diana's name. She rushed to my aid. It could be the fish we ate earlier, she said. No, Diana. It's my mother's germs that have infected me. In the kitchen later that night, I drank herbal tea. I chewed on diced ginger to soothe my stomach. But I needed to talk about my mother's idea of love. Her words were my passport to confusion, to a nightmare, but also my vehicle to a history I could call my own. Would you own all your history? I asked Diana. Most of the history we know is not told to us by our people but taught to us, Diana said. Most of our parents are silent about our past, and I understand. Because what's history to us is something that they've lived in real time, and endured its pain and humiliation. You're lucky your mother left you her diary. Diana made me another cup of tea. I wish my father wasn't as silent, she said. I know his silence was there to protect me, but in the end, it left a gap. I carry a big hole, and like anything with holes, it's bound to leak something precious from within. Sometimes, we need to decide what's more painful: to tell our stories in all their colours and shapes no matter how repulsive they might be, or to accept the cost of untold stories. Diana paused. She rested the side of her face on her hand. After a while, she lit a cigarette. I tried my best to do my own work, Hannah, she said. I travelled to collect as much as I could from what my father and ancestors went through. After I graduated from uni, I worked various jobs, saved money, travelled to Ghana and Jamaica, talked to relatives in Yorkshire and London. I found stories that were so complex I wanted to run from them. They were not all about resistance. In my family, there were freedom fighters, slaves, lovers, workers, abusers, preachers and sex workers. And I wanted to know not just the story of their defiance but also how they courted each other, made love, how they brought joy to their lives and the sound of their silence. I want all that's mine. I want all that my ancestors endured. I want their garden of thorns and flowers, of violence, of intellect. I own that garden and walk in it, even if it means bleeding. Diana poured wine for herself. Hannah, your mother's words are yours, even if, as you say, they're full of germs. Diana fell quiet as if the history blowing through her gathered load. A long moment passed. Oh, I'm tired, she said a while later, and as she stretched her arms, yawning, her breasts slipped out. She had a tattoo of an anchor between them. I read the symbolism. None of it made sense as images unpacked themselves in my mind, one after another. I'm going to bed, she said. I stayed in the dining room, stared at the wall in silence, then fell asleep on the chair. I was woken when the front door slammed shut. Anne? The smell of chips filled the air. Anne stomped upstairs, and a while later, I stuttered behind her. I turned the handle of the bathroom door. Can't you see it's fucking busy? Sorry, Anne, I said. I'll wait. Anne grunted. Her sighs swept away the mountains of tension that had gathered on my chest. When she came out, our eyes met. I couldn't determine whether the scent of oil, burger and fries came from her skin or the work T-shirt she had in her hand. What? You haven't seen titties before? It's nice to see you again, I said. OK, cool, she said, swaying to her room in her skirt. She turned, hissing: Stop staring, perv. I bowed. I squatted on the toilet seat when Anne flung the door open and entered, mumbling, Me and my fucking forgetful mind. I pressed my legs together. She grabbed an earring from the sink and was about to leave when she paused. She tilted her head, examined me and left without saying anything. Next morning came, then afternoon, and a cold evening found me in the dining room with Diana, talking, smoking and drinking. After she shuffled to bed, I was back in my room with my mother's diary. *Friday. 5 a.m.: I made it a habit of mine to gift Xehay something special. Every now and then, I treated him to the flower between my legs. As he stared at it, I imagined what it must feel like for him to see it and not be able to penetrate it. But that hunger fuels the obsession behind his attention to detail. I appreciate the beauty of being looked at without getting touched. I can't express the kicks I get when I tie him to a chair and then dance naked in front of him. I couldn't have imagined the depth of pleasure I'd feel on seeing so much passion in the animated eyes of a restrained body.* I remembered Diana's words as I put my mother's diary aside: Own your history, Hannah. I sat on the windowsill and scanned London, imagining where Anne liked to dance, party and have sex. I pondered when it would be my turn to fall naked in arms and get dressed in lust. I returned to my mother's diary and read some of her words, which gave deeper roots to her in my world. *Friday. 10 p.m.: Xehay and I had a talk earlier. Years have passed since we met. After he painted my nails, he held a mirror as I applied lipstick. I told him I would go out with someone else tonight, pressing my lips to even out the red lipstick. He massaged the sternness between my eyes like a rock pressing on my nerves. These headaches. This disgust at the world and everyone in it manifests into a fire that I can't help. I'm always enraged. It's as if I'm a steam train needing the coals in my firebox to burn to make even the slightest move. I spat into his mouth as if I would set fire to his submissiveness. I slapped him. He held his screams. I knew he enjoyed pain. I knew he enjoyed pain. But recently, I realised that there's more to it. He's been working and looking after his family since he was nine. He didn't have a childhood and never enjoyed his teenage years. With me, he wants to be young again. I'm surprised I'm not mad at being used as a form of escapism. The fact that he's not as passive as I thought makes me beam. I'm probably developing a soft spot for him. After finishing my make-up, I asked him to dress me for my night out. As he opened my wardrobe, I smiled. He's different from all the men I've loved in so many ways. Anyway, I'll marry him tomorrow.* The diary fell out of my hands and crashed to the floor. I wrapped my arms around my chest, rocked back and forth. Would my illiterate father have given me my mother's diary had he known what was in it? As I shivered in my bed in my room in London, with my mother's diary on the floor, the images of my parents in an occupied Keren stayed in my mind. O. B. B. Who am I? Am I like my mother or father? Can I carry both of their traits? And will I break if I carry their varied sexualities and desires? So many questions, but that night, as I picked up my mother's diary, I brought it close to my chest. With a stagnant present and future in London, my past mattered more. It stormed. With the rush of water through the pipes alongside the exterior wall of the room, sensation surged through me. A tinkle ignited my toes, and excitement engulfed my entire body. I dreamt of Anne, as if the way to remove my mother's actions from my mind was through more scandalous behaviour of my own. I knew little about Anne apart from the few details Diana had told me: that she was adopted as a child from my part of the world and escaped her adoptive parents' home at a young age. Anne was due to arrive home soon from her work. I touched her in the odour of grease she left on the staircase, in the bathroom and in my lungs. I was imagining chewing her fingers as if they were the fries at the restaurant where she worked, when I heard her voice. For fuck's sake. I opened her door. What are you looking at? At you, I said. Well, don't, she said. I'm in a free country, I said. It'd be nice to give people their privacy, you know, she said. I do what I want, I said. Don't you think it's annoying you're in my way all the time? Can I help you take off your jacket? What? I want to help you get comfortable, I said. What a weirdo, she said. Fuck you, I said. Say what? Fuck. You. She hurled herself at me. I gathered her in my embrace and faltered backwards inside my room on to my bed. On top of me, she pinned my wrists to my mattress with her hands. Rain dripped from her hair onto my face. She was the sky raging – clouds clambered on top of each other inside her. Her eyes were full of darkness. She rained on me as her drenched jacket flooded the pit of my torso. I wiggled. She straightened her back and took off her jacket, one arm at a time, after which she placed a hand around my neck. I moaned. She took her hand off and undressed. I was dizzy and drugged when she gave me her ass. I parted her cheeks, and there it was: metaphors like bonfire exploded in my mind. When I stretched her further, it was as if her hole was a secret cave of Pompeii, the walls of her skin filled with art, and, with it, a prophecy of an imminent demise after a short-lived pleasure. Fist me, she said. I hesitated. Oh my fucking lord, you don't know what that is, do you? She jumped off me and pulled off my jeans. Let me show it to you, she said. Two fingers. That's all I could take without pain. But I needed pain to drown all the pain inside me. I grinned. You like it rough, don't you? It was as if the black panther bolted from her door and possessed her, her eyes as golden and her claws as sharp: Here, she screamed. And here. A time came when her hand searched for tales inside me. Stories beyond the immigration stories. She explored me until I saw my humanity shining in her eyes, the eyes of a Londoner. Anne made me visible through sex. But I was more than seen. My inside was her mirror onto which she beamed fragments of her past, of herself when she was young before life roughed her up. Our bodies are all we own to remind us of the hope we've lost, the home we will never have back. Home has become something beyond a land. Home is your bellybutton, Anne, I said. Home is your breasts, your eyes, your smile. Home is the gap between your teeth, the dent on your thigh, and the birthmark on the back of your shoulder. You are my home, said Bina-Balozi on that bench in Fitzroy Square. O B B, you are my home, I said, as I ogled the *O* I expanded to fit me and all my memories. One night, after we wrestled until my defeat and I succumbed to her claws, I was on all fours and Anne sat behind me. It's like I'm seeing more of myself inside you, the more I open you, she said. It's like my childhood, my family who gave me up for adoption for a better life in this country, have all been buried inside you. You're a sorceress, a witch, she said. I wanted to tell her I was neither of these things. She saw what she wanted to see. Sex, the way we did it, offered this possibility, to find something concealed inside us, to find things that many take for granted. *O*. O B B, give me your *O*, let me see the constellations of the father, mother, aunt and country I lost. Out of breath, Anne collapsed in my arms. When empty of fire, she surrendered to her tender side, which I nurtured in my embrace. I caressed her hair, hummed a song in Tigrinya for her. One night, like many other nights, Anne crashed on my chest and fell asleep in my arms. I can't remember if it was me or her, but one of us whispered *I love you*. Sometimes love becomes a war, and war yields love. Anne snored softly. But the scratches of her nails and the scars of her love burnt and kept me awake. I crawled out of bed and headed downstairs. Jazz music played from Diana's CD player in the dining room. Diana was on her feet, eyes closed, hair loose and arms folded across her chest. I assumed her soul was dancing to jazz, as she had once told me. I stood next to her and hoped that mine would join hers in a long dance. But nothing in me moved, as if the tunnel to my soul was blocked. I was about to sit when I slipped and hit the chair. Diana carried me to the sofa in the living room. What happened, sweetheart? She rested my head on her chest. Why don't you have your clothes on? She pulled a throw blanket and covered me with it. Memories that acquired the shapes of humans lodged in my head, turned into spectres that haunted me. Ghosts I met here, those who followed me from Eritrea, and those who climbed on my back, held on to my arms and hid in my skin's pores across the desert. Spirits of those who had died found an oasis in my chest and used my body as their passport to the West, and when I arrived, I looked like an overloaded lorry about to tilt off balance. I sunk my nails into my scalp and skin as if I could pull these people who searched for a home in me out one by one. I longed for the days when my head was filled with the sound of bombs and my eyes with the reflections of fighter planes. Every day that I waited for the letter from the Home Office was one more day without belonging here, yet in the process of waiting, I lost touch with my country. Rootless, I dawdled away my life by the window. My days disappeared as fast as the Jubilee line. I wished I hadn't destroyed my passport. But would my people have me back when I was this perverted, when I had discovered the shape of my interior in the eyes of a black panther? Diana hummed as she caressed my head. I closed my eyes and fumbled with my mouth on her chest decorated with necklaces and searched for something to calm my breathing. I found her breasts. I latched onto her nipple and sucked. Hannah, what are you doing? Stop. I didn't. Hannah, gently, sweetheart. Hannah, I can't breathe, said Diana. Thinking it was my body that weighed on her lungs, I attempted to move and let go of her breast. No. Don't. Please stay, she said, as she slid her nipple back between my lips. I floated into a dreamlike state and fell asleep. I divided my time between having sex that resembled a war with Anne and migrating with my bruised body to the oasis of Diana's chest. There was nothing else I could do. I had to remind myself again and again that I couldn't study or work until I had received a decision on my application from the Home Office. Hopefully anytime soon now, my lawyer said. I waited. I was on the verge of turning nineteen or maybe I had reached my twenties already. Diana had vowed to let me stay until the decision letter came. I cooked Eritrean food for her: fried meat with berbere we bought from an Eritrean shop, and chicken stew. She made dessert. Cheesecake was my favourite. I loved to watch how she made it: her chest lifted when she squeezed lemon, as if the tropical fruit brought memories of fields of Ghana and the Caribbean. Her chest was full of fields. We spoke about that. About repeated metaphors. We often thought about the moon, the sun and the tropics, as if to keep reminding ourselves of our roots. Through this repetition, we found a language apt enough to give a voice to the forced silences inside us. We have been chained. Clichés are potent weapons of the dispossessed. I can't remember who said that, but does it matter? Every night I clung to her breasts, I consumed her ideas and plucked from her garden of thorns, roses and platitudes, reclaiming our metaphors to redefine them the way we wanted. She recalled an anecdote with a lover. Or a lover-to-be, I should add, she said. I say that because love and sex are different, as I discovered to my dismay, and I was convinced he would be my lover. One night, we were in bed. He stabbed me from the back as if I was an enemy he'd waited years to corner. No rhythm, but full of fury. I pulled myself from the knife on his thighs. History has been unkind to us. It sought to erase us through violence, and I told him that I need tenderness to make me whole again. She knelt, and as she opened the oven door she burnt her knuckles against the grill. She screeched. Ouch. I held her hand and blew on it, the condensation of my breath cold as if the soon-to-arrive winter emanated from my chest. But you can't know the joy of fire if you haven't experienced coldness, and you can't feel the warmth if you're not frozen. Thank you, sweetheart, said Diana, adding, with the oven still open so the heat blew out against my legs, Hannah, I told you that story with that man to say I needed what you did the other day. I know you've seen my soul. I'm 53 and I still have love to give. Life is short, and I don't want to take all the love I have

with me to my grave. She paused and lowered her head.
We both averted our gazes from the moment, from what
was between us, because we didn't want to label it: was it
refugee–native, teenager–adult, Eritrean–English, or something else? Did it have to be labelled? But that was what it
meant to be like us, always probing, always doubting, like
the White and Blue Niles travelling alone, negotiating
obstacles, going through a survival phase, between drying
and flooding, between high and low, night and day, until we
met at a confluence: her house in Kilburn. One night, Anne
lay me on my back and tied my legs and hands together,
to better access the Africa she had missed since she was
adopted. I remember thinking about how reductive we were
becoming. Yet I opened further dimensions of my body to
her longing and imagination. That was what sex was to me:
for someone to fuck me with their imagination in the way
Anne did. She made her room inside me. Sex is a home for
some of us who find ourselves on the road, who journey
parentless without rest, living from one colony to another,
fleeing from one war to another and searching for freedom.
Sex is our freedom, I thought, as I saw BB's shadow, hesitation growing on the roses of Fitzroy Square behind him. I
longed to press him deeper into my thighs, to convince him
that his search for a home would end the minute he let me
inside him, because our bodies were all we had control of.
Everything we need is inside us, I said to BB. I lived through
loving, and sometimes the pain reminded me of an otherwise
strange life. Diana slid the tray back inside the oven after
making my favourite cake again and pulled me by the arm to
her breasts. My journey in her house wasn't about learning a
language or adapting to a new culture. The language I learnt
fast, though the misplaced words, heavy adjectives and

meaningless phrases added to my confusion, for those who were born into the language didn't know what it meant to adopt words. I had no culture to adapt to. My culture was universal, one that travelled between Diana's books on her shelves and the ones my father collected and buried. Words are my culture, I said to her once as I sat next to her on the sofa. She had been laid off because of back problems. That was what she'd told me at the time, although later, after her death, weeks after baking that cheesecake, I'd discovered that she had left because of harassment. She didn't tell me this information because she wanted to shield me from losing faith in a country I had fled to for peace and a better future. She wrote in her suicide letter that she wanted me to make my own judgement about my new country. The country she loved and hoped I'd come to love. She apologised for not showing me Yorkshire as she promised, for not taking me to the Lake District, or Edinburgh, a city that gave her the confidence to fall in love with melancholy. Her drinking started when she was forced to quit her dream after failing to find any acting roles for years. She became despondent about how the free world around her tried to shackle her ambitions. Yet, Diana wrote, what's freedom when it's founded on prejudices? She wrote all that in her last letter. A letter a part of which I had tattooed on the side of my back, for everyone who comes to my bed to leave with a snippet from Diana's world. Letter by letter, sentence by sentence, as if my body were a medieval scroll. My body became a memorial to her like hers was to her ancestors. I discovered the body's power as a carrier of narrative the night after Diana slipped the cheesecake into the oven, and we sat on the sofa in the living room. When I noticed her toenails were painted yellow and her fingernails pink, I remarked that she came close to resembling a painting. Oh, wait, I'll show you, she said. She stood and pulled down her trousers. Flowers covered her thighs. Tattoos of roses met her lilies, orchids and hibiscuses. A tropical garden on her skin that gave me the fragrance of longing. How much yearning can somebody have for their ancestors? My God, Hannah, you get it, she said. Because some would ask, why tattoos of flowers? They're such a cliché. She pulled up her trousers and sat back. Originality is in the details. It's in the interpretation of things. The problem is that we translate texts, images and situations through the perception of others, not our own. That makes something a cliché. Own an interpretation, and you own a new meaning of the world. That, Diana said. Then she pranced over to the shelf and returned with a book. With my chin on my palm, I studied her. Shit. The cheesecake. She ran to the kitchen. I looked at the book she had left on the sofa. I removed it and sat in Diana's place as if I could bathe in her warmth until she returned. And when she did, she came back with waves of smoke floating behind her. The cake was as black as charcoal. I have nothing for you to eat. I'm sorry. She sat next to me and pulled me towards her. I sunk into her body with each suck from her soul. We slept on the sofa. We woke up. We talked about the pigeons under the bridge and the number of times their poop had landed on her head. Life's been shitting on me for a long time, she said once, as she sipped her glass of wine. And as I fed from Diana's breast, I devoured the love in her chest, the wine in her breath, the sadness in her thoughts. London slid down my throat with the imaginary milk from this Londoner. I was a citizen of London, a city that existed on the map of her chest and on Anne's thighs, and, I hoped, in Bina-Balozi's bottom. O Bina-B. I bit Diana, revitalising the heart that was about to fall silent when it had so much love still to give. Hannah. Our souls dance to the jazz. Diana threw her head back, and I was about to close my eyes as she did when the smell of fries drifted towards me. Anne. What the fuck are you doing? I can't believe this. Anne ran upstairs, and then later that night she left Diana's house. The street is better than staying at a whore's home, was all she said to Diana. *Everything passes, love remains – Kullu yihalif, fiqri yit-erif.* Diana and I were left alone in the house. Weeks passed. Silences piled on top of each other like a tower block, inhabited by our sadness and by unspoken desires that had to be abandoned. Bina-B became more prominent in the wake of Anne's departure. In the clear air of my silent days, he rose to life, in small memories wedged to the furniture he left, and in his shadows in the cracks of the walls. In the weeks after Anne left, Diana and I kept our distance. I spent most of my time in her living room reading books about history, poetry and art. We cooked for one another. We ate without talking, and our thoughts festered in our shadows, reposed against the walls of rooms dimmed into serenity. We drank without seeing each other, as our mouths puffed clouds of smoke between our faces. On the occasions the smoke cleared, sucked out by our lungs, she cast her eyes low, and wrapped a scarf around her chest, concealing the lakes of love inside her. Overnight, we orphaned each other. Jazz music blurted out from her CD player. We laughed when we encountered funny stories in the papers we read. We groaned when a text brought a memory that stabbed. And we were revolted at the turns life could take, in that dining room, in that house in Kilburn, when we closed ourselves to the world. And it did. Letters arrived for both of us with news. Diana's letter came from the police days after Anne left, saying complaints had been made against her for inappropriate behaviour. Investigations were pending, adding to Diana's mounting debt to an ungrateful society. The mountains on her back grew steeper. Mine said that my application for refugee status was rejected. The person who read my story at the Home Office found it unconvincing. Unconvincing, I repeated. Although my story, heavily edited by my lawyers, stretched their imagination a step too far, they couldn't send me back yet, since the war between Ethiopia and Eritrea was still ongoing. Instead, the Home Office granted me the status of an asylum seeker, which, as my lawyer explained, meant they'd take their time to decide on my case, which meant living longer in the waiting lane, the slow lane of London, paved with fear, which meant more uncertainty, more anxiety, more pressure on my mind. I remembered the donkey on the slope of the mountain in Keren. *Everything passes, love remains – Kullu yihalif, fiqri yiterif.* I reread the Home Office letter in front of Diana, who had folded her letter from the police and put it on top of the pile of letters, queries, bills, frustrations. Deportation was a possibility that hung like a noose next to my head. Whisky. Give me whisky, please. And wine. I put my letter from the Home Office in my bra and made my way to my room. I drank alcohol but was reduced to faltering by a life that refused to open its door. Like a photo I'd crumpled into a ball and straightened out, London would be a wounded dream from then on. The London that I had imagined living on the Jubilee line, travelling at speed, now tottered in my head as if on a broken track, each wheel pressed on a tongue from a different country – Serbia, Somalia, Ethiopia, Peru, Iran or Eritrea. I thought the man by the window was right.

London was full. It could no longer hold me. I was too complex, my story unbelievable, untranslatable. What London needed was someone who would fit in immediately, without too many traumas weighing on their spirits and productivity, someone who came with a laughing box to brighten moods in this overcast city. I gaped through my window. Londoners' dreams gathered into a cloud that roamed the sky and threatened rain. I thrust my head further through the window. To spend the night under the downpour of Londoners' dreams is to risk encountering a city on a march with a knife in one hand and a magic wand in the other. Soaked, my hair heavy with rain, I imagined Anne fucking her lovers somewhere else, breathing in from someone else's hole, discovering a new kingdom and continuing a hedonistic existence after her work at the fast-food restaurant. I, we, the immigrants, remained locked into permanent indecision over our status, our future and our self-esteem chained to a probability of acceptance or rejection, kept hostage to insecurity. Anne was the explorer of our inner worlds. That night at Diana's, I took my mother's diary and placed it open against my chest as I lay in bed. It was as if her words took on the shape of wings. I know I've used this metaphor before, but I make no apology. Words are my wings. I imagined myself flying over London. Not the London made of buildings, roads, canals and places of worship, but the one built with stories. I could see words like invincible rivers flooding the city. I could see stories like pillars on whose shoulders the city rested. I could see skyscrapers written against the grey sky. A city that lasts and glows like London is built on words, not concrete and cement. I travelled from Eritrea to seek a safe place to live. I came to London alone, accompanied by my story, which accumulated new words and new twists along the journey. Yet what made me suffer, what made my body ache with torment, was what led the Home Office to dismiss my story. But had I not, in the first place, reacted in the same way to my mother's story? Had I not found it hard to believe that an Eritrean mother imagined a type of love that could inflict wounds? Was I the child she made for my father that I read in one of her entries? *Tuesday. 4 a.m.: Last night, Xehay sat between my legs, ogling my inner thighs all night. I knew in the morning he would wake up to a world in the shape of my vagina, as impregnable as our love. But then, an hour or so after we went to bed, he screamed. He had a nightmare every night now. Mary, save me, he said. Please save me. Let me guess, you had a dream where dogs chased you, I said. No. Not dogs. But I was chased by children, he said. Children who looked like birds and flew everywhere. Everywhere. Oh, Xehay, my dear husband, your dream is to have a child. I'll make you one.* I couldn't bear to read her diary any further, to imagine I was a birth of terror. A whole day passed with me in my bed, staring through the window, listening to the squeal from the rail tracks and watching the occasional sparkling light flashing onto the darkening sky. A plane gliding low brought the memory of when I was on one, floating above the clouds of the city, its fog parting like curtains, welcoming us to its vast runway. At 10 p.m. I lumbered to the bathroom. Sorry, sweetheart, I'm going in, Diana said from the entrance, wrapped in a white towel. I must get ready for a date. But I won't be long. I nodded and trudged to the kitchen. I made myself English tea, not in the way Diana taught me but the one I discovered for myself: milk first, followed by a tea bag and a spoon of sugar. I prepared my dinner and sat at the table to eat my cornflakes with milk when Diana came into the kitchen whistling her favourite song. 'I Just Called to Say I Love You'. She repeated the song a few times as she moved around me, opening and closing the cupboards. Hannah, have you seen the olive oil? I need to shave my legs, and I've run out of gel. It was in my room. Why? she asked. I couldn't tell her about Anne's fist. I lied. For my hair, I said. I'll get it for you. Could you please bring it upstairs? She left the bathroom door ajar. I caught her reflection in the mirror. It was as if the fluorescent light in the bathroom had excavated a different angle of her chest. She rubbed the scrub, moved her hands in circular strokes around the breasts I hadn't touched in ages. I returned to my dinner with the image of Diana fixed in my mind. I watched snooker on TV. A Scottish player won the World Champion- ship again. When I made my way to my room, winter found me lying on my bed. I closed the window and sat with my bare back on the ice. I shivered down a lane of memory. How ridiculous memory becomes when you're sad. Like a rope you grasp to save your sanity, but then discover that its strands are made from the same sadness engulfing you, like a noose around your neck. It was my first, or perhaps my second or third, English winter. For immigrants, who don't own their time, seasons are imaginary. There were two books on my desk that Diana had bought me the previous Christmas. An Irish novel and one about nature. I selected the latter. It was about trees. Did you know that you can make trees talk back to you? Did you know that trees have laughter? Did you know they're the poets that give rise to the tides in the oceans? Did you know you enrich nature when you make love under a tree? Trees grow on sentimentality and bloom on melancholy. Some of those in Bloomsbury inherited Virginia

Woolf's sadness, and others migrated to the mind of Audre Lorde and sprayed my nights with erotic dreams. I discovered all this from conversations with London trees when I became homeless and lived under mine in Tavistock Square months after that evening when I switched off the snooker game and found ice sprawling in my bed. Diana came back from her date sooner than she'd wanted to. Her date turned out to be a disappointment. I joined her at the table to talk about it. He kept staring at other women in the Indian restaurant, she said, at the dinner table. Like men, he loves women's asses. Well, I love men's asses, I said. How was his? Diana guffawed, and after a moment of silence, she added, Sometimes, I overanalyse my situation. Perhaps this is it. I need to accept that I might never find romance, but I'm still surrounded by things I love: my wine, books, cigarettes, London, a long, warm shower, and... She paused. Then, with a broad smile, And you, sweetheart. Diana caressed my hand. I'm sorry, I said. Nah, don't be, she said. Anyway, I left him and fled to a kebab shop. She tucked strands behind her ears as she unwrapped a kebab and chips. Eat with me, please, sweetheart, she said. The chips reminded me of Anne. I heaved as I swallowed sorrows with the memory of her squirts. When I picked a chip and a fat-drenched slice of kebab meat, my inner thighs throbbed. Grease had historical relevance to me because of its association with desire. The histories of the senses, intimacy and passion were as relevant as those of nations. I thought of my mother, who wrote her own story. To her, her history was as important as her country's. But owning your story could have consequences, as Diana would show me. That night, as we shared her chips and kebab, Diana reminded me again that her pain weighed less than mine. We were trapped in a cycle of mutual empathy. Look at me blub in front of you, she said. Again. It took me a while to register what she meant. How do you measure wounds? I didn't ask why she thought my sorrows were worse than hers and, in turn, more deserving of sympathy, a thought I'm sure crossed my mind often, and I might have said it a few times already. For a second that evening, though, I was proud that a mountain of pain on my back was a molehill. *Friday. 3 a.m.: Xehay came home from work to find me in bed with another man. I asked him to come over. I saw tears in his eyes, though I was sure they were happy tears. He always wanted a child, my darling. And it was going to happen tonight. He sat in bed. I caressed his face. I love you, he said. I love you too, I said. I parted my legs to the man I chose to father my child. Xehay leant forward. He kissed me as the man put my legs on his shoulders and slowly entered me. That was the night I conceived Hannah.* No. Silence. No. *That was the night I conceived Hannah.* No. I ran to the street. No. I sprinted aimlessly, this side, the other side, through dark alleyways, cul-de-sacs and mews, and I stood in the middle of the road, and later under the bridge. *Xehay is my father.* I panted, gasping for air. *No. Xehay is my father.* I returned to Diana's door breathless and covered in pigeon droppings. I screamed my father's name. *Xehay.* Xehay is my father. It's not the other man. My father's name is... I paused. Yes. Yes. Xehay. My father's name is Xehay. Shut up. People are sleeping. It was the man opposite Diana's house. *Xehay is my father.* He leant his head through the window, and glowered: Put a sock in it. I was convinced he was related to the officer who cursed my grandfather. Nigger. Rats. Refugees. Black. I picked up a stone and darted towards his window and hurled it at his head. Blood. Another stone. Bigger. A pool of blood. He pressed charges. Prison. A record. My path to British citizenship was ruined. Days after my imprisonment, I had a visitor. It was the caseworker who brought me to Diana on my first day in London. He gave me an envelope and a box. I'm sorry, he said. I'm sorry. Diana was gone – as if my presence had kept her alive. If I'd known, I wouldn't have reacted to my mother's diary in the way I did. I wouldn't have thrown those stones at the man. I'd have been there putting a lid on her wounds. Diana left me a gift. *A box of gifts for life, my sweetheart*, she wrote in a note, scrolled a smile and a wink at the end. There were two thousand pounds and a letter in an envelope. The envelope felt heavy. Weighted by words and her parents' pictures, which she wanted me to have. I carried part of her story with me: a Londoner whose heart was where young people and their stories from different parts of the world met. *Everything passes, love remains – Kullu yihalif, fiqri yiterif.* I moved to a hostel in Victoria, a few doors away from an old French woman and her dog on a leash. The dog barked at me when I stood in front of the hostel with a facade like a cloud. Don't worry, the dog is not racist, the French woman said. Animals never are, I said. But are you? She pulled the leash and dashed away. I rested my head over a pillow that stank as if stuffed with shit. I held my bag with my clothes, the letter from the Home Office, Diana's box and my mother's diary in my arms, carrying more stories, as if that was what life was all about: humanity's spines made of tales, anecdotes, incidents, words. I turned my head from side to side. The bag was as heavy as a rock on my chest. As I sobbed, moans raged through the thin wall that separated my room from next door. I trembled, my breath grew shallower and my vision blurred. Fuck me, the woman next door screamed. I sat up. I needed to be with those having sex to drown the sorrows inside me. I left my room and knocked on my neighbour's door. They quietened. I banged on the door harder. Who the fuck's that? It's me. Who? Me, Hannah. Not now, the man said. I heard a thud and the sound of items breaking. I wanted to be in their room to break and be broken. Open, I shouted, and thumbed both fists on the door. Fucking hell. He stood there, chest naked, wrapped in a towel. His Adam's apple moved on his throat like the hump on the camel that smuggled me out of Eritrea. As if he would help me escape the torture I was feeling, I pulled off his towel. I knelt and sucked his condomed dick. Who is she? What is she doing? Mark, please make her stop. My mouth relished the fruit of her vagina. Mark, make her stop. The woman stormed out of the room. Mark rolled on the spotted carpet that already stank of piss. I sat on his face and added mine to his mouth. The police were called. Mark refused to press charges, but I was thrown out. Thank you, Mark said outside the hostel door after the police had left. I've been bringing lovers to this hotel for years because I wanted to experience something transcendental, he said. I thought, ah, I thought I'd never get there, but, ah, then, ah, then you came... Out of nowhere. I'll never forget how that made me feel. I didn't say anything. Will you be alright? he asked. Yes, I said. Do you have a place to go to? I looked at the street, the trees, the thick clouds that darkened as they seized on to more storm, madness, and Londoners' passion. London is my home, I said. I remembered that first day I looked at London from the back seat of the black Vauxhall that took me to Diana's home in Kilburn and noticed the men sleeping on the street. I'll find my room somewhere on its streets, I said to Mark. That's what I used to say when I used to sleep rough, he said. Here, you'll need this, he said. I remembered Diana's roots in Yorkshire as I put on the Northerner's overcoat with padded shoulders, a rose pinned to its lapels, and his yellow fedora. My mood turned as if Diana latched on to her roots in the geezer's clothes, and my memories of her crawled to my skin. We became each other's extension, like Langston Hughes's skin was an extension of the night. It was instinct that led me to my next home in London: a tree in Tavistock Square. I didn't choose it. I was led to it. After I was kicked out of the hostel in Victoria, I walked around London. A few days passed with me wandering about, catching sleep under bridges and next to abandoned buildings. Late one morning, I entered a red telephone box and called Diana's landline, which she had placed in the living room by the bookshelf. There was no answer. I rang again, as if she was in her chair in the dining room with her wine and whisky. No answer. I read her letter while in the phone box, then left. Roamed around the streets. One rainy day, I found myself at a junction outside a hotel opposite Russell Square. I looked through the window at a banquet on a long table with cutlery, glasses and flowers. I pressed my hands on my stomach, turned around and gave my back to the buffet. Instead, I feasted on the beauty of a woman in a wheelchair, dressed in all black, holding a bouquet of roses. I darted behind her as she sped down the road, and followed the red roses through the heavy black rain. The woman arrived at a park, where a lover threw himself into her arms. The two fell silent and kissed. Wet London rode their tongues. Stirred, I leant against a tree trunk and sat down to shelter from the rain. I fell asleep. When I woke up, I walked around the tree and inspected it as one would a new home. The exposed roots made the tree as exhibitionist as Anne, and the thick trunk made me feel I could lean against nature in the way I'd given my back to my father on that bike journey on my last evening in my hometown. Its branches were as wild and varied as the thoughts in my head. This was my new home. I slept on a cardboard box I had fetched from a local supermarket. My mind hurt as if it were the one that lay on the bare floor. I hid the money Diana had left me and her letter in my bra and used my bag with my mother's diary as my cushion, so that her words became the source of my nightmares and dreams. One afternoon, I spotted a book on a bench. I walked over to it. I picked up the book by Cummings and returned to my tree, leant against it and read. That book accelerated the relationship between me and the tree as I read one poem for me and another for the tree. Sleeping under a tree watered with London rain and fed by the lascivious poetry I read out loud made it the most nourished and free tree in London. It danced throughout the night, slithering with its leaves through the darkness laden with memories and haunting harmonies. This tree turned into a hub for other dead poets who loitered about Bloomsbury. I counted up to 100 poets who became regulars. It was midnight when, while reading my mother's diary, I spotted an enormous figure in a flat cap and a light blue suit, surrounded by flowers. He wrote with green ink on the black sheet of the night, and his words, like birds, flew about the park: love, indignation, infatuation nestled around me. Soon after, Pablo Neruda dived into the ocean of his words. He was a poet who couldn't swim in his own creation and was about to be pulled under by the current of layers in his lyrics when I dived after him. Having saved Neruda, I was about to return to my reading when T.S. Eliot swaggered into the park with a group of poets as if he were a guide, and pointed out to the new residents of Bloomsbury the places where they could rest. I chuckled when Eliot told his fellow poets that to live in London as an outsider was to aspire to nothingness. It was later that night that Jonathan Swift followed me to my toilet behind a tree at the far end of the park to write 'The Lady's Dressing Room'. He showed me how the imagination becomes a sifter of disgust, and I smiled as I lay in my bed of cardboard box and recited his words: 'Oh! Celia, Celia, Celia shits!' The following morning, a woman with grey hair and a green button-fronted sweater presented me with a bag of books and a folding chair. I'm leaving Bloomsbury after thirty years, but I don't want to displace these books with me, she said. Will you accept them as a gift? I received more free books from a second-hand bookstore and from the frequent visitors to the park, who would leave their books next to me instead of spare change... *EYES: Hannah can't sleep... her room is London... she can't switch off the light... she tries to think of a solution... Hannah covers her cardboard-box bed with a blanket... and goes for a walk... streetlamps glitter everywhere... London looks like Michael Jackson on the set of Billie Jean... Hannah laughs... she turns into a street... a fight... blood... vomit... a muddy footpath... overflowing bins... piles of chips next to a telephone box... she wanders into another street... boutiques throw flashes of luxury brands... The many faces of London bring unbearable confusion... Hannah sprints away... back to her tree... she searches for a poet who will bring darkness to her inside so she can sleep...* I was sitting on my new folding chair with my yellow fedora pulled forward, reading a book, when the sky squalled and the rainstorm brought a woman with red curly hair into my path. I hope you don't mind me sharing your shelter, she said, a cigarette in hand. My eyes raked over her. Inspired by her blue shoes, I said. Anyone who wears the sky on their feet deserves all my respect. She crooked her head towards me and grinned. Her eyes matched the feelings I held inside me. Her smile, though, was as bright as her shirt. The mismatch between her appearance and the feelings I detected led me to ask: Why are you sad? Who said I am? Your eyes, I said. Well, you either aren't as good at reading eyes as you think you are, or my eyes are too complicated. I stood and tipped my fedora to her. If I had a kitchen, I'd have invited you to tea, I said. I could do with some of your intellect. She rolled her eyes and mumbled a thank you. It's not a problem, English rose, I said. She protested: That's clichéd. But in that London park on a summer afternoon, the rain lifted the fragrance of flowers from her freckled skin. Besides, I'm Irish, she said, smiling. Sweet smile. Again, she resisted the compliment. She shook her head and said, Goodness, you're unoriginal, aren't you? I exist to fight against originality, I said. She raised her eyebrows and lifted her hands. Fine, at least I hope you'll remember this encounter in an imaginative way. Anyway, I need to go, okay, she said. She stretched the y in okay. Her mouth held on to some letters of the alphabet for a long time. After the Irish woman left, I returned to my books, debating with Neruda about the repetition of love as a consolation in his poems. *Love is as insignificant as air to a dead body*, I told Neruda, quoting from my mother's diary, something that must have repulsed him because I did not hear from him for some time after that. And later that night, I came to blows with the spirits of Langston Hughes, Dorothy Parker and Anna Akhmatova when they turned their backs as I masturbated after re-reading a poem by Cummings. Poems are not porn, they told me in unison. I tell you, there's no force like that of dead highbrow poets hurling words at you. But in my defence, the slightest reference to love or the body threaded on the page with poetic language stimulated my libido in those days. And in those days, I made love to and with my senses because the language of the poets came in touch with the language of my interior. That day, after the Irish woman left, I thought she wouldn't remember me any more than those clouds that one remembers for their mysteriousness when they break into raindrops. But she came back with the afternoon sun the following day. I'm not escaping rain this time, she said. I came to say hello. Her name was Dr Róisín, a lecturer at a London university. What was it that made me love London those days in Tavistock? Was it my encounters with people like her? Was it the endless walks I had taken with a wounded soul that endeared me to this city – as if a city's idioms, flavours and nuances of history and stories need open pores to seep through? I ceased to be homeless, since I now found home in London's arms, a company in its air, and friendships among its trees and flowers. I slept on a bed made of a cardboard box, but in my mind, London slipped a hand under my back every single night, why would I otherwise not feel pains or ills? I took that delusion encouraged by the dead poets like a sleeping pill before bed. One morning, I took a stroll around London while wearing prescription glasses I'd found on a bench in the park. Dizzy, I returned to my tree with a deformed perception of the city when Dr Róisín came with a blanket and clothes. But it was when she brought a dish of lamb and sweet potato shepherd's pie, based on a recipe her mother used to make every St Patrick's Day, that the Dr and I spent an entire evening by my tree. I insisted she take my chair as I sat cross-legged on the grass, moisturised by summer dew. I lit a cigarette and leant against the trunk of my

tree. Dr Róisín took a lip balm from her bag. She smacked
her lips after she used it and asked me if I wanted some.
I declined as Róisín brushed a strand of red hair from her
face. Behind her, on a bench by the entry of the park,
Virginia Woolf balanced a pad of paper on her knees. In
front of her, Orlando and Mrs Dalloway stood with a 'Do
not disturb' sign. A ladybird landed on Orlando's shoulder
as Dr Róisín lit a cigarette. A man in a yellow jacket led by
his dog with its leash tied to his waist swaggered past us
and pumped his fist as he rocked to a stereo playing music
in his hand. Some of the benches were occupied by people
reading, others by those who stared ahead of them in
silence, as if they'd come here to walk their thoughts in
the company of strangers. A nurse in a light blue uniform
with navy piping inched through a gate from one of the
nearby hospitals, holding the arm of a patient wearing
a gown. Around them a group of boys scattered, laughing.
I was about to turn my attention to Róisín when a mother
giving a piggyback to her child stumbled. I rushed to help
her, but she shouted: Do not touch me. I returned to my tree.
The fragrance of flowers travelled through the air. Róisín
kicked her heels off, lifted her legs off the floor and folded
them against herself. She sighed and gaped at me. Róisín
was on my mind the morning I awakened from a nightmare
to find myself covered in roses. It could've been a romantic
fellow dweller who spent the night arranging the roses on
different parts of my body, but I suspected it was a work
of nature, stirred by the poets living on its dark mews.
I collected the roses and placed them behind my tree...
*EYES: Outside the garden, Hannah spots a family of two adults
two children and an old woman... they're wearing traditional
Eritrean clothing... talking in Tigrinya... Hannah follows them...*

they laugh... she laughs... they talk loudly... she mimics them... the old woman notices Hannah... Hannah stops and bows her head... the family picks up the pace... Hannah does the same... they laugh again... Hannah does too... they all stop and look back at Hannah... Hannah wants to tell the woman the saying her father taught her and that she came with to London that is as valuable as her belongings... but Hannah can't remember the phrase fully... ኩሉ ይሓልፍ... she translates it in her head into English... everything passes... love remains... she tries again in Tigrinya... Kullu... fiqri... Hannah can't remember... she screams... the old woman comes towards her... Hannah runs away runs runs runs runs... Róisín turned up on her bicycle one Saturday morning. She asked if we could spend some of it together. I sat on the crossbar of her bicycle, and she zigzagged through the park and through the university square where she taught. When we arrived in Regent's Park, we disembarked and strolled on foot, and we decided to get on a bus when Róisín told me that sometimes she liked to grab a bus to its last stop to dream and think about life along the way. After she parked her bike and locked it, Róisín and I stepped onto the number 18 on Baker Street, behind a couple who had been running in the park. Their odour conquered the bus, which we took all the way to Harrow. On the way, Róisín talked about her husband, where they had met and the ups and downs of their relationship. That day, Róisín invited me to move in with her and her husband. I'm not ready to leave my tree, I told her, without revealing my main reason. I loved nature more than people, and I couldn't leave my tree, the poets nestling in its branches. Róisín could see nature tattooed in words between my breasts, which she'd had a glimpse of when I changed into a crop top as green as her eyes that she'd gifted me one sunny day, along with toothpaste and a toothbrush... *EYES: Hannah is horny... meets a man... so you're a refugee right says he... it depends on what you mean by that says Hannah... I mean you fled a war says he... yes yes but I also fled many types of war says Hannah... I'm confused says he... me too says Hannah... well that makes two of us then says he... yes but you started the confusion says Hannah... I don't understand says he... me too says Hannah... well this is meant to be our first date says he... that's what I thought too says Hannah... I guess we're not going anywhere with this then says he... be my guest says Hannah... peace they both say to each other... Hannah goes back to her tree and makes love to herself...* Once, I walked with Róisín to a jazz bar near Camden that she frequented without her husband because this was where she treated herself to silence, to music. The high heels stretched her body. I had to look up to find the reflection of her sleeveless sequin dress in her eyes. The side-swept hair made it look as if her alone time was formal, bound for a red carpet. Róisín laughed and confirmed this observation when she said, True, there's this glamorous side to me that comes out when I go out on my own to be with myself. Her words made me think of Diana, who often took a book to a bar. I shared this with Róisín. This reminds me, she said when we arrived at Warren Street station and paused by a newsagent kiosk that was closed. She gave me a book. Seeing what it was about, I asked Róisín whether every Irish person read these types of books as if to nourish their dark sides. Your dreams must come dressed in gothic style, I said. Oh, please, Róisín said. Assumptions, assumptions. A motorbike zipped through the traffic, which had come to a standstill, in the same way that thoughts raced through my crowded head. Red busses rubbed against the branches of trees as if trying to set fire to both London's skin and mine. It drizzled. How many times London burnt me before its rain soothed me. How many times London's wind uprooted me from a point in life, only for its breeze to smooth my landing onto another. Róisín took a folding umbrella out of her handbag, linked our arms and continued. I was walking Róisín to her bar, but London was walking me to many places. London was like a mill grinder that had taken me whole and turned me into fragments. The fragrance Róisín wore for her night alone with herself reminded me of her presence. She squeezed my hand and said, Hannah, one day, you must come to one of my house parties. I promised her I would. I was thinking about parties and people and dancing that morning I sat on the blanket over my cardboard box in a vest and boxer shorts. My eyes followed a bird that somersaulted mid-air, and returned to earth and to my body, resting on my belly button, full of acrobatic energy... *EYES: Time ticks away tick tick tick tick tick tick tick... we see it on the watch on Hannah's wrist... the long hand and short hand moving in circles... one second added to Hannah's life then one minute then one hour then one day then one week then one month... repeat... one second then one minute then one day then one week then one month ... repeat... one second then one minute then one hour then one week then one month... repeat... we're following the hands on her watch to the point of dizziness... we remind ourselves that we're the eyes of Hannah... eyes that acquire the skills of feeling and seeing... and we feel the passage of time in Hannah's thoughts and mind... time becomes a reminder to Hannah of the reasons she fled to this country... time brings memories of ambitions and dreams thwarted... time accumulates and presses against her chest like a boulder... she tries to sleep... finds weed... sleep, sleep, sleep sleep sleep sleep sleep... then she wakes up... time ticks away... she strolls aimlessly... shadows of Londoners glide across trees buildings cars people... a city of silhouettes on the move... big shadows... thin shadows... fat shadows... short shadows... hunched shadows... shadows of walkers and their dogs... shadows drinking shadows thinking shadows in tears shadows dreaming shadows sighing shadows heaving shadows depressed shadows in contemplation shadows of terminally-ill patients shadows of pregnant women shadows of politicians pondering a decision that would change their lives and no one else's shadows of office workers about to terminate a contract and fuck up someone's life shadows of women in hijab shadows of young people carrying their parents' divorce papers shadows of birds about to fly from nests of someone else's aspirations higher higher higher towards cloudy sky we're all things that will disappear with the storm... Hannah goes to sleep... wakes up... time reminds her of her aunt and relatives in her hometown in Eritrea who patched together their savings to send her to Europe to flee the war and do something meaningful to support them... she smells memories that cook on her bones and tastes as if sewers are strewn on her skin... yuck yuck yuck...* Róisín came to see me under my tree with coffee and croissants. Hiya darling, she greeted me. How's your mood today? she asked me. My mood is like summer, I said, full of sunshine, warmth. I whirled as I added: and like flowers, smiles, longings and dreams. Ooh, please hold on to that feeling and come with it to my party, she said. I did. I took my shower in a shelter and stuttered along to Róisín's party in a plumber jumpsuit I had found in a charity shop that went well with my fedora. She opened the door. I stood still, as if I no longer knew how to enter a home. Noticing my hesitation, Róisín pulled me by the arm. Come, darling. We were in an embrace when her husband surfaced behind her. His hair danced over his shoulders to a fan that pumped air through the narrow corridor. He shook my hand, swaying it about. Your curly hair tells me you're an Ethiopian, he said, still by the door. No. I'm Eritrean, I said, and it's crucial you know the difference. He protested: It's as if I killed your mother. The Ethiopian army did, I said. Oh, I'm sorry, he said. Me too. Silence. But we're all the same, Hannah, he said. All Africa is one. They divided us. He pointed at Róisín. I thought it must have been unintentional as he retracted his finger when she said: I'm Irish. What the hell are you on about? Róisín stormed off to the living room. Róisín? I called. As we followed her, her husband said, You see what I mean? She managed to turn my sister against me. He cackled. It was a joke. I joined him in his mirth, hoping this would get him off my back. But no matter how hard I turned my pupils away, I could see him growing in my vision. He was here. There. Everywhere. He was a traffic warden at work and, it seemed, at home. Róisín pulled me away from this typical London room with a low ceiling. In the kitchen, we stood by a grazing table. Her breaths flamed the fire in my mind. I picked a slice of ham with cheese. Róisín played pop on a stereo placed on a table behind her. We toasted our friendship formed on the streets of London. She spoke above the clink: Cheers. I congratulated her on her recent accomplishment: winning a contract for research that would soon take her to Kenya and Uganda. Thanks, my dear, but God, how I wish to have success in my private life too. Róisín stared at the door. It was ajar, like my life itself, giving me glimpses of inspiring moments, like now, in the London flat of an intellectual couple. She tensed her jaws and rearranged the finger food, glanced at me in silence and licked her fingers. She dimmed the light. My fondness for the silhouette of a human curved against a moment of confusion goes back to when I learnt to make love to myself. You'll understand me because you know what longing for something is, she said. I thought we promised no politics, I said. We're in England. Róisín snickered. I placed a hand on hers. I feel you're holding back something, I said. I sometimes hate him, she said, blurting out spit that I licked from the top of my lower lip. Why? I asked. She sat on a chair and crossed her legs. Maybe hate is too strong, she said. But my friends tell me I'm a person of extremes, so maybe it's not. I don't, I said. I had no idea why I had this rush for Róisín that was as sexual as the first time she had come under my tree on that rainy day. Perhaps I confused her invitation to her party for a date, or I was aroused by her gaze, which obtained a new meaning in a London home rather than the street. As I leant towards her, the pulses of her fury stirred me. I had heard about the Dr's marital problems on the number 18 bus and during the various times we'd met. But she now spewed more issues, which clogged her airways like pieces of bone. He hardly listens to anything I say, she said. And he doesn't share much with me. We meet in bed, we make love. But no matter how great sex is, it can't be a substitute for conversation. She continued: Talking is sexy. Ideas arouse me. I feel he doesn't talk because he's hiding something from me. She paused. Róisín, do we need to know everything about each other? I asked. Róisín picked up a napkin from the table and wiped her mouth. I see what you mean, Hannah, but the silence frustrates me. I didn't understand. I thought she'd told me she loved silence. I told her this, and she replied, Yes, but there's a type of silence that brings sadness, Hannah. He invites me to ponder over what he might be feeling, but without ever knowing the accuracy of my interpretations of his state of mind, since he doesn't talk, I'm left with questions and thoughts about him. I was thinking about her convoluted statement when she added: Where's the joy in that, Hannah? I had no answer. Let me put it this way, Róisín said. It's not knowing much about him that hurts me. He's open-minded and driven, she said. But I hardly know anything about his childhood. I want to know what made him the person he is. Róisín rolled her shoulders and shook her arms as if to loosen up the awkwardness I detected in her voice. Hannah, he's the love of my life, but it's like I'm married to a mystery box. But Róisín... I paused, as if searching for what to say. And, Hannah? Róisín, he's your husband, not a piece of research. Róisín put her hand on her chest and said: Gosh, darling, I hope I'm not giving you the impression I'm snoopy and a control freak. It's not that, Hannah. I like to know because I have a long history of being forced to live with secrets. Those years of suppressing the real person inside me taught me the dangers of suppression. She mentioned suppression a few times, and then we returned to staring at each other in silence. I spotted a dot on the surface of her eye as if her freckles had invaded her body inside out. I caressed her neck. I didn't expect this would be calming, she said. Veins between my thighs expanded into a bulge as those in her neck loosened up. With my breath tinted by the garlic-marinated prawn I had chewed minutes ago, I leant towards her. Her man barged into the kitchen to announce that visitors had parked their cars where they shouldn't, as if the traffic warden in him had gone into overdrive. The couple argued and I followed it with interest. As she told me on the bus, he was an educated man who found himself supported by his wife because no British company valued the degree he had obtained back home as much as they did hers. Her power over him was clear when she grabbed a handful of crisps and said to him: Chillax, babe, this is my party, and I paid for everything, don't ruin it with your anxiety. I imagined that in his head he was calculating the pros and cons of winning the argument. He couldn't afford to lose her, and the 70 per cent plus, Róisín told me, she'd put into the household pot since he was studying for a master's in agricultural studies, which raised her doubts and suspicions about the longevity of their relationship. His future was drawn with his homeland in mind. I grinned when he dropped his chin. I winked at her, exited the kitchen and visited their bedroom while they were occupied with welcoming their guests. It was painted white. On one side of the bed lay books on computer programming, agriculture and food, floor to ceiling – his, and on the other side there were books on philosophy, economics, literature, notebooks, cream, an alarm, Vaseline, shoes, scattered newspapers and magazines – hers. My excitement rose when I spotted a pink double-penetration dildo under her pillow. I made my way back to the living room to find it packed with a few people high-fiving each other, some blowing kisses, and hugging between men who yelled cool slangs of Yo sup, Howudoin mate and What's the craic? My favourite, though, was said to the men: How's it hanging? I looked at my thighs, which looked like a new room yet to be furnished for you and you alone, BB. O. Bina-B. A gulf of nations brought together in that tiny space: those who came for networking opportunities, others for a laugh, and those who searched for love and sex. I thought it was my turn to add to this chaos. I held Róisín's hand and was about to waltz her to her bedroom for a talk when she said, First, meet Armani. Armani, in a dark blue velvet blazer, velvet trousers and a flat velvet cap, lifted my hand and kissed its back. I snatched my arm away. We won't be long, I said. He attempted to place my accent. Between a recent arrival and a seasoned Londoner, he concluded, not knowing the deceptiveness of immigrants' accents, like waves many of us ride, gliding and jiving as we move between the estuary, cockney and posh, something a native couldn't or wouldn't do. Oh, we can do many things with this tongue, I said to him, sticking it out, long and pierced, drawing my host's nervous laughter. A woman in braids intruded into our mirth and kissed Róisín on the edge of her mouth. The singer turned towards me, and as she kissed my hand, her pink lipstick left a mark on my skin. The man in velvet protested and feigned rage at a woman stealing men's signature charm. The singer pouted: Ooooh, poor you. The circle extended and became more circus-like when a wannabe comedian approached with a cuppa and took the conversation the predictable route of How do you take your tea? I rolled my eyes. Each person interjected. The cacophony of voices became a symphony of the city. The singer included me in the conversation by asking if we do it another way in Africa. Well, I'm Eritrean, I said. And a Londoner, I added, and the crowd around me cheered, raising their glasses, bellowing like hooligans: We're Londoners. Londoners. Londoners. Soon after, Róisín and I made our way to her bedroom and sat on her husband's side, as if assuming his place, beginning a confession that I liked her. I have enough problems for now, she said. I'm not saying you don't, I said. Crazy, she said, when I told her that difficulties are the foundations upon which all passionate and memorable sex or love is built. She reminded me of her age, double mine. Like a house, a body holds memories, and I make love to the self and its reflections of its past, I said. Lord, she said. Let's go to the living room, darling. They're waiting for us. Wait, I said. I recited a poem from memory: *Had I the heaven's embroidered cloths, / Enwrought with golden and silver light, / The blue and the dim and the dark cloths / Of night and light and the half-light...* Róisín interrupted me. Don't do this to me, Hannah. Moments passed with the two of us holding hands without speaking. Here, said Róisín. I want to show you something. From a bag under her bed, she pulled out a picture. Sitting back next to me, our shoulders touching, she said: Look at this. I was a seven-year-old boy and about to receive my first communion in Dublin. Days after this was taken, I told my parents that inside me, I was a girl. They didn't believe me, and told me to keep quiet. They built walls around me: walls of silence, fear, lies. I lived through those years trapped inside a cell that nobody else could see except me. Everywhere I went, I was inside that cell, at school, working student jobs and at family parties. As if my bones were rotting, I was falling ill all the time. And for what? To live someone else's truth instead of mine? So years later I moved to London and started my transition, and here I am: this woman in front of you. That's why, Hannah, I can see all your sides. I noticed it the first moment I looked at you in Tavistock Square. We're seers, darling, because we had to see ourselves the way we are from the inside first, from the moment we were born, before we learnt to see the rest of the world. We're the seers, I repeated her words. I bowed. Róisín raised my chin with her fingers, her eyes like a book that led me to imagine chapters of her history she'd told me passing through them. We are stories of fragments until we see ourselves the way we want to be seen. We are the seers, I mumbled. Yes, we are, she said.

Silence. Let's go back, she said. Back in the living room, we danced, ate, drank, flirted. One observation at that party startled me. It didn't have to do with anyone or anything that was said, but it was about London and how it moved between the guests in those tight spaces in that tiny flat, which was different to my observations on the streets. London took over the shapes of the guests' bodies, residing like the glint in their eyes, the rhythm in their throats and the beats in their souls. London evoked their spirits, ideals, dreams, disappointments, resurfaced with the stories they told, and wore their death, like the death of the man who kissed the back of my hand, the man in velvet, who died weeks after that night at Róisín's, where I made love to him on the sofa in her living room. The guests left, the Dr and her hubby retreated to their bedroom, and the Englishman and I stayed behind talking, taking turns on a bottle of white. Jazz played on the stereo, and London danced in the corner under the arched floor lamp. It was as if London was an incarnation of Diana. It moved like my foster carer: head bowed, swinging side to side in a slow, absent-minded way. I smiled. The old man and I chit-chatted about this and that – the guests and what they wore and how they talked, who had a hard-on and why – until I downed the last drop of wine. The man complained. You finished it. Man, you finished it, he repeated it. Don't cry, I said, and pinched his cheek. He closed his eyes, his head swayed. Don't die, I said, chuckling. You laugh, he said. But I see death. I see it. Oh, come on, don't be a miserable old git. I see life in you, I said, and placed a hand on his hard crotch. This here must have a life of its own, he said. I unzipped his trousers and took his cock in my mouth until its head tickled the back of my throat. And as I sat on Armani's cock, rising and falling

to the last wind of life in him, I heard moans. I plucked
my nipple out of his mouth and staggered to my feet. Hey,
where are you going? Shush, I said. I'll be back. I tiptoed
my way to the Dr's bedroom. I peeked through the door.
The husband and his wife, Róisín, lay on their backs, legs in
the air, the soles of their feet kissing. When they interlaced
their fingers, it was as if they pressed a launch button:
the double dildo wedded them into a levitation by means
of mutual pleasure. They floated high with my spirit.
They moaned. It was on that long pink rubber that their
relationship trod. It was a bridge on which what was unsaid
between them, emotions, ideas, doubts, anger (many words
floated in my head), ferried them from one side to the other.
Without it, I imagined a collapse. I stepped closer to their
bed and sat next to Róisín on the floor. Róisín rolled to her
side. Hannah? I finished reading the poem I recited to her
at the start of the party: *Had I the heaven's embroidered cloths
/ I would spread the cloths under your feet: / But I, being poor,
have only my dreams; / I have spread my dreams under your feet;
/ Tread softly because you tread on my dreams.* I returned to
Armani in the living room and found him snoring. I covered
him with his jacket. I put on my fedora and walked home to
my books, to the night, and climbed my tree to seek the
company of poets, who grew to 101 when James Baldwin,
who stopped over in Bloomsbury on his way to Paris,
joined us. Baldwin stood in front of me and shook his head.
How marvellous, he said as he examined my fedora. I don't
remember but it could be then that I stole from him the
fichu neck scarf as he lay asleep next to some poets I'd
rather not name... *EYES: Hannah buys a porn magazine from
a sex shop on Tottenham Court Road... she rips out the picture
of a man in a chastity belt and uses it as a bookmark... she reads*

Samuel Beckett's Not I... and Beckett's MOUTH *and we Hannah's* EYES *look at each other in... silence... Beckett's* MOUTH *and we say at the same time: Is This Love At First Sight... silence...* MOUTH *agape...* EYES *wide open... then... shoooooooooo... bang bang bang... guns... sky brightens... fireworks... Hannah... can't sleep... can't think... can't rest... can't eat... can't drink... more bangs... hello Hannah say the police... hello says Hannah... policeman and policewoman nod in harmony... it's been a long time says the policewoman... yes it has says Hannah... so how have you been doing says the policewoman... today I'm fine says Hannah... good to hear says the policewoman... but you can ask me about yesterday morning says Hannah... well shall we just stick to today says the policewoman... as you wish says Hannah... have you by any chance seen or heard any disturbances this early morning says the policewoman... no unless you mean the disturbances that happened in my head says Hannah... no Hannah not that says the policewoman... then I can't help says Hannah... are you sure says the policewoman... yes says Hannah... OK says the policewoman... but the policewoman adds... Hannah if you remember anything do not hesitate to call... call how says Hannah... aha yes so don't worry about it says the policewoman... see you soon says the policeman... later says Hannah... Hannah can't rest... can't sleep... come on up here Sister Outsider says Audre Lorde...* One day, I was at a charity shop in Notting Hill when I spotted a dark blue velvet blazer, velvet trousers and a flat velvet cap. They were the clothes of the old Englishman whose life I had tried to prolong with sex at Róisín's party. As I paid for the set of velvet, the shop manager bemoaned the passing of his friend, who had lived alone following the sudden death of his wife. He had known the English couple for years, since they bought the velvet set. Years of stories and friendships started over this piece of fabric, said the manager, and now it's back here. Everything is inheritable by strangers in London, including the past of the couple and the man's attire, which I wore the next time I met Dr Róisín for breakfast at a greasy spoon near her university to talk about her forthcoming research trip to East Africa. Armani would've been pleased to see how beautiful you look, she said as she hugged me. We ordered our food and drinks. My eyes lingered on Róisín as she gathered the set of salt and pepper with her hand and added a bit of both to her plate of eggs benedict. I placed my flat velvet cap next to my plate of full English breakfast. What's on your mind, darling? By now, she had renamed me her darling. In the first letter the Home Office sent to me when I was at Diana's, they rejected my application for refugee status. But in their second letter, which was brought to me by my caseworker when I was in prison, they granted me the less prestigious ranking among those seeking refuge, and one I liked for its complicated construction: Exceptional Leave To Remain. That was me: not here nor there, not a refugee, but someone with no home, someone with the right to stay here in the UK temporarily, meaning that if Eritrea got its independence, I might be sent back. That Home Office letter linked me to Great Britain in the way that the pink dildo bridged Dr Róisín's body to that of her husband. I rolled with it and embraced this life of ambiguity. For the years to come, I'd be known as Hannah, nationality: Eritrean-Exceptional Leave To Remain-Potentially-British. And to be a darling meant I was a citizen of this Irish woman's heart, in the way I had been of Diana's. Róisín repeated something she'd told me about her country, this time locking her eyes into mine, as if the backdrop of Eritrea's history mirrored hers. Róisín and I met each other in our histories of violence, famine, migrations, the death that we saw many times en masse and embedded in our veins, yes, the Dr and I met each other in our languages that refused to be refined, in our dark sides that wouldn't be confined to the nights, and instead dwelt in our minds twenty-four-seven. Róisín and I made love by reading each other, probing at all the words and thoughts written in the spaces between our eyes. We were lovers in the way that characters in books written centuries apart can be in conversation and love with each other, with distance and time deemed irrelevant when the heart can travel across them all. I don't know why, but as I sat in front of her, I remembered a moment with my father when I was seven or eight, sitting in front of him in our garden as fighter planes roamed in the sky above us. Should we go to hide, Father? I asked. He didn't answer. I looked up. Father, the planes. He'd fallen asleep. My eyes darted around the greasy spoon. Construction workers occupied most tables, their gear scattered around them on the floor. As if some memories are hazardous, I pined for their earplugs, face shields, hard hats and reflective vests. We ordered more drinks. Róisín sipped on her tea, and watched me over the rim. I have something for you, she said, and put her cup on the table. Look, Hannah, I know you told me you weren't ready to study, but I've researched everything for you in case you change your mind. She took an envelope out of her bag. If you ask me, you're ready to go straight to university, she said. But I was told it'd be better if you do an access foundation course for a year and then go to uni. Voila. Simple, ha. What do you think? I didn't say anything. Here, take this envelope, darling. Everything you need is here. Róisín and I strolled to Hyde Park holding hands, in silence. We parted company and I returned to my tree and the poets.

Everything passes, love remains. In the envelope, Róisín also left me cash to rent a place until I sorted myself out with accommodation and food. As I left my tree, I thought about choices, why we make them and how they make us unhappy most of the time. I thought of studying engineering as a way of remembrance, a way to ensure that I wouldn't forget my aunt and my relatives who had sent me to London and the goals they had hoped for me to achieve. But people blurred and faded into ambiguity with the passage of time. How ironic, though, that my mother, who died when I was still a baby and who I only knew through her diary, was the most memorable. I became convinced by the power of word and art to form and cement memories. This thought led me to study Art and Humanities, majoring in literature. I collected my bag on that last night under my tree and awoke all of Bloomsbury's poets. I had prepared a speech to thank them when Neruda returned from his absence through the tunnel of one of his verses, and recited a poem that amounted to a warning: *If You Forget Me... If suddenly / you forget me / do not look for me, / for I shall already have forgotten you...* I put on my fedora and wrapped my arms around the bag that contained my mother's diary, Diana's letter and Róisín's envelope, and I made my way out of Tavistock Square... EYES: *Hannah fixes her fedora and sits next to Sappho in the clouds... when she sees Diana and her parents passing each other in the galaxy Hannah stands up to wave... she slips through the clouds and falls back to earth... oh my head Hannah screams... oh my stomach... she holds her side and faints... good morning Hannah says the nurse... do you remember us says the doctor standing next to the nurse... Hannah shuts and opens her eyes... the good news is no one hit you this time says the nurse... but the bad news is you fainted says the*

doctor... Hannah I'm afraid we'll have to do some bloodwork says the doctor... we're concerned... OK says Hannah... Hannah do you have a next of kin contact says the nurse... yes says Hannah... brilliant says the nurse... I need to write down their names and contact numbers says nurse... Neruda says Hannah... OK says the nurse... his phone number... actually not Neruda we just had a big row but you can put down James Baldwin Audre Lorde and Virginia Woolf says Hannah... I missed that could you repeat says the nurse... none of them says Hannah... I'd prefer you to call Borges he has cute cats... can his cats come here says Hannah... the nurse and the doctor look at each other... Hannah I'm afraid no pets are allowed here says the doctor... the nurse coughs... ahem... Hannah I'm sure Borges can be a great next of kin I like him too but we need real people says the nurse... anyway you need treatment Hannah says to the doctor... Hannah sleeps... wakes up after an operation... she feels something inside her is missing... she doesn't care... absence is the wind that fans her fire... she's discharged from the hospital... she returns to her tree... she puts on the prescription glasses she found on a bench weeks before... she wanders around London... that deformed perception of London makes Hannah laugh... ha... ha... ha... Hannah sings... always look on the bright side of life... nothing will come from nothing, ya know what they say... cheer up ya old bugga c'mon give us a grin (always look on the bright side of life)... O Bina-B. O. B. B.
I looked around Fitzroy Square – as if the rain had washed the facades off the buildings, its environs seemed like relics of a lost world that only made sense when the poets buried in the air of Bloomsbury reappeared and draped the square with their words. The silence around Bina-Balozi broke when Rimbaud and Verlaine sauntered from their old lodging in Camden Town and joined me on the bench with their absinthe. Soon after they'd got through their bottle, they

quarrelled. Fearing it would descend into another violent episode in their relationship, I was about to shuffle away when I remembered their splendour was inseparable from toxicity. As if the thoughts in my head about Bina-Balozi inspired the French poets and lifted them out of their doldrums, Rimbaud undressed and Verlaine painted his lover's asshole in words. The air of Fitzroy Square, loaded with the ambience of bohemian life, wafted from their poem about the anus. O Bina-B. BB became the chorus of a song. O B B. I tipped my fedora to the French poets and was about to disappear with them for a stroll around Bloomsbury when BB spoke in a whisper. Hannah, I worry. Of what, BB? That I'm a man, and I... Maybe I should have let him finish his sentence, but I interjected: I'm not a stove, BB, your manhood won't incinerate in my lap. As if caught by surprise, he stared into the distance. Puddles formed around us. The wind whipped up. The trees swept into frenzy. A cacophony of rustling leaves filled the air. BB coughed and cleared his throat. Hannah, is... is it about power for you? I tilted my head to the side: What? This, he said. This what, Bina-Balozi? He pointed to my thighs. I breathed in the night, and the trepidation I heard in his voice. I'm sorry, Hannah, he said. Words squeezed through him as I imagined I would into the mouth of his thighs. Hannah, you see, I came to this country to find peace. But I've never had it. Even though I've never encountered the violence I've seen back home here. But those doubts, Hannah. The suppression is real. I live as if I've also smuggled my family from my country in my mind. Every time I want to do something that makes me happy, I stop. Wearing a thong under my suit is the easy part. It's the undressing of my mind that I find so difficult.

How do you do it, Hannah? I didn't expect to assume a role similar to that of the customs officer who received me at the airport on my arrival in London. I had no key to heaven. BB stepped closer. Hannah, how did you embrace the real you? I wanted to tell him that reality is just a function of what we imagine – and I wanted to remind him that imaginations are genderless wombs. But I didn't wish to be drawn into his struggle. I know what it's like to be someone like me, oscillating between joy and sorrow while assuming multiple identities, leaving a beloved aspect of myself behind to embark on a new adventure with another. It feels like there are arrival and departure halls all over my body, and I spend a lot of time in them bidding farewell to one version of myself and welcoming another. Dimming part of myself to give a glow to another part brings joy and sorrow. I enrich and wound myself by this continual flipping between the sides of myself – the feminine, the masculine, the submissive, the dominating, and the nothingness – yes, being nothing but to exist is an orientation I embrace now and then. Although I didn't say any of this to BB, part of me longed to hold him, open his back, the door to his obscurity, listen to the songs I imagined chirping from the birds hanging on his ribcage. I looked at the pool of water in the distance, and as if I saw an ocean with ships on the mud- puddle, my imagination sailed into the bay of BB. Moments passed with me tongue-tied, transfixed, staring at his face, which acquired the shape of a star, like that of my mother, father and Diana. I shuddered at the thought. As if I wanted to hold on to him, no matter how unearthly all this felt, I talked. Bina, I said, we've crossed deserts and seas to come to this country, but now we must take the riskiest journey, the one that matters most to us. BB, we're not in Europe on a quest to find alternatives to our countries lying in ruins but to construct our own in the island of our lust, I said. I don't understand, Hannah, he said. Are you equating sex to a country? I didn't know whether his question was genuine or had a hint of mockery about it. But who are we, I thought, if we don't savour our ridiculousness, our madness, in the way we embrace sanity? *Everything passes, love remains.* The rain in Fitzroy Square intensified. Some of the poets ran for cover, and I imagined them sheltering in Bina-B as if his body were full of caves. I saw him as a poem engraved in the cavity of the earth. Was that part of the reason I couldn't pin him down, part of the reason I saw that making love to him would be largely with me taking the active part, leading my army of desires to dig inside him, to excavate the rhymes that he possessed in the well of his emotions? Some had to be restrained to love, I thought. I dreamt of him so often, so much, for so long that I had no idea if he was as I imagined him: someone who walked among the poets, who dared to write verses with his body. My mind oscillated between seeing him and losing him. I wanted him to speak more, to eradicate my impression of him, break through the walls of the ideas and fantasies that shaped his persona in my mind. His silence and the few words he said reminded me that when we migrated to this country, our lives became part real and part illusion, caught between our true selves and the stories we had written in our Home Office application, that we had censored and polished to gain a sympathetic ear. I wanted to share with him my belief that to be refined and subtle kills the mystery of living. These thoughts made me sound pretentious, a trait I had recently vowed to remedy. It's hard, Bina-Balozi said after a long silence. What's hard, BB? To believe you're real, he said. Strange, I said. Earlier you told me it wasn't easy to give in to your desire to be with me, and now you're questioning my existence. Do we have to make sense to each other? We both sighed, we both hunched up, enveloped by the night, the rains, by our desire. Uncertainties firmed inside me. I had imagined this encounter with BB to be fleeting, but so intense that it would etch its way into permanence in my memory. I had imagined riding with him on the wings of madness, gliding through the clouds of lust, roaming with the souls of poets buried in the air of Bloomsbury. But here I was plunging deeper into my thoughts. My feet itched. Leave, a voice on my mind urged me. And I was about to when BB said, Hannah, can I sit? I shifted over on the bench. I hate getting wet, he said. Let me get wet then, I said. He didn't move. Looking at my lap, he asked: Is it there? Oh, yes, I said. It is, as it has always been. It only became visible to me, you, and the world now that I'm ready to share it. I spread my legs as if to confirm to him that what nestled between my thighs wasn't a foreign object in the way I was to this country, but something that had roots as any other organ in my body. BB stretched his arm towards me. The rumbling I heard, as I took his hand, was of hearts in mid-flight, of our passions like swords cutting through London's clouds. O.B.B. Bina-B let go of his umbrella, our eyes locked, and in that instant something changed – his hesitation evaporated, and certainty anchored inside him as he lowered his torso onto my lap. I was about to unzip his fly when he raised his head to scan the deserted square populated by poets that I could see and no one else. Stop, Hannah, he said. BB, I said, we're black. We obtain visibility when we're on the verge of breaking the law. This is our moment to shine. He chortled. Not here, he said. OK, follow me, I said. We climbed over the gated garden fence and headed to a bench in the middle of the flowers. He perched on the bench. I promenaded around him. His ribs poked out through his delicate skin as black as night. His back dipped at his bottom and rose like the mountains of Keren at the tail end of his spine. I didn't come to his body to conquer but to love. Not to shed blood but to reach the peace aplenty inside him. The bones of his pelvis rose like columns shielding his penis. He was smooth, and the only bit of hair on him veiled the round of his anus as if he was guarding it even from his own urge to see. I knelt behind him and ogled his anus the way a poet's pen stares at the first blank page of a virgin book. Moments passed. Contemplations, thoughts, images swam between us in the air. With his ass spread over the night, his hole threw shades of dreams into my chest. I gave in to the lure of carnality. O… Bina-Balozi. BB. Bina-B. I sat on the bench. He spread his legs over my lap. I could feel him smiling in the light that travelled through his skin and flowed like electricity in his veins, illuminating his body in my arms, the deeper I was inside him. O. B.B. Bina was cocooned as if he had found his throne. I grabbed him by his waist. He rested his head on my collarbone. My fedora was like a roofed veranda under which our breaths curled like smoke. We both cried. We had arrived. We have arrived, said Bina-B. The poets of Bloomsbury rose as if to compose a poem in unison. But Bina-Balozi was the poem. I, his writer… I smile. I dash out of Fitzroy Square. The poets urge me not to leave Bloomsbury, and BB wants me to stay inside him, but I'm a wanderer, a migrant, a refugee, an exceptioal-leave-to-remain, a traveller drifting between ideas, thoughts, lovers and countries, and for a second I wonder if I've also been moving between life and death. I sprint away from Fitzroy Square, and behind me Bina-Balozi is humming a song. O.B.B. His voice sharpens my spirits. I run. I find myself on the South Bank. Music is everywhere, on the pathway, next to a film café, inside the Royal Festival Hall. Music is the umbilical cord between our city and our lives. There are all sorts of music next to jazz. Latin, West African, Middle Eastern, Indian and Persian, as if the world comes to London to sing, experiment and reimagine freedom that at times looks as thick and murky as the water of the Thames. I notice a man playing a Peruvian flute, with its tip dressed in the same rainbow colours as his bandana. I spin my fedora on my head and push through the throng. I give the Peruvian a tenner and ask him to play jazz. I'll try, he says, as I'm trying to live life in London like the jazz displaced from a saxophone to the flute in his mouth: not from here, not from there, hanging on the tip of improvisation. I move to the music as Diana taught me. I tilt my fedora and dance with my soul. I remember her words: *We all have a dance floor inside us and our souls are the dancers of our feelings.* The crowd erupts in laughter when the musician waltzes towards me with his flute, stirring the beasts in me, the wounds, the history, the love. Dance, my darlings. Dance, I plead with Diana, Anne, my mother, Róisín, my father, and all those who clung to my collarbones as Bina-Balozi did when I entered him on that bench in Fitzroy Square, when he flung his arms around my neck and climaxed into a trance as I impregnated him with a new idea, a new vision of love and sex. A thought comes to me. Rooms and the memories we create in them, whether in a building or inside a lover's body, whether at Diana's house or inside BB, are the same: they're tombs for reflections of our fragments. Like my mother, I give air to all my fragments,

no matter how small or big, disturbing or acceptable.
Who are we? asked Bina-B on the bench of Fitzroy Square.
Refugees with stories unconvincing enough to be granted
British citizenship? I titter now: how can they believe
a story like ours, a story that keeps reinventing itself
because we have accepted to be born and reborn in the
womb of an imagination? And imaginations are genderless
wombs. I remember that lunchtime when Róisín came to
my tree to spend her break with me. It was raining, and
I was combing the sadness from Virginia Woolf's hair
while watching Verlaine and Rimbaud explore each other's
bottoms before composing 'Sonnet du trou du cul'. Virginia
and I chortled as the French poets read it to us, and I
recounted the French poet's words as I opened BB's *O* in
Fitzroy Square: *Dark and wrinkled like a violet carnation, /
It sighs, humbly nestling in the moss still moist from love.* I was
inhaling the wild and musky nest of sobs of the French
poets when Róisín greeted me. Hello seer, she said, emphasising to me that once we learn to see inside, we acquire the
knowledge to see the supernatural world where the poets
of Bloomsbury resided. She reiterated this in the greasy
spoon before her departure to Kenya and Uganda. Dance,
I tell myself as the Peruvian man plays his instrument.
Dance, I say to the spirits travelling with me. The armies,
the Italian fascist soldiers, the smugglers, dictators, rapists,
the lovers, the English general screaming nigger at my
grandfather while my grandmother was giving birth to my
mother while her stomach was bound with flower-and-
butterfly-print fabric. Let's dance, I say to the memories, the
past, the future and the supernatural that resides between
them all. Dance, I exclaim as the Peruvian musician who
had come with his band from his hometown in the Andes,

living in the strands of his hair, echoes my words. Dance, he says. And in Spanish: *bailemos, querida*. I experience the duende. And as I attain Lorca's heightened state of passion, of emotion, I step over the rail of the Thames to cross to the other side, to move towards the decision I have crafted in my head, to write my story as it is, unlike the censored version that dwells in the Home Office building. The Peruvian's voice grows hoarse as he blows melodies louder into the instrument. He tilts his head and directs his flute towards the sky, as sparkling as the skyline of Bina-B's inner thighs. His tunes like pearls scatter on my path on which I skid down the bank into the Thames. Dance, I say to the seers. Dance. The sky roars. It pours. The river laps its water around my neck like a black scarf. The London in me is about to leave with my soul. I guffaw at a memory of that first morning on Diana's doorstep when she wiped the pigeon shit off my shoulder and raised her eyes to the man leaning through his window across the street and mumbled *Twat*. I laugh so hard that my yellow fedora falls off as I fold and swallow water but not enough to sink me. Just as well.

Acknowledgements

London: thank you. This book is for you.

Thank you to my agent, Jessica Craig (for your dedication and for fighting so hard alongside me to ensure this book was published the way it was conceived in my imagination), Jess Chandler (it was lovely to find you and Prototype, and I appreciate the freedom you gave us), and Michele Hutchison (who even offered to edit this book if no publisher was willing to publish it). Thanks, too, to the wonderful Aimee Selby, Anderson Tepper, Lucie van Rooijen, Rory Cook, Martin Colthorpe, Jurgen Maas and Literatuur Vlaanderen.

Thanks to Étangs d'Ixelles, Brussels. For years, I've been coming to these ponds to read poetry to the water, trees, flowers, nature, and the air. One day, the ponds and nature gifted me *The Seers*. That day was in March 2020, during the first COVID-19 lockdown, when I stood in front of the water and pulled out my iPhone and the word Hannah popped up in my mind.

It took me three weeks to finish the first draft, which I wrote entirely on my iPhone. This book could only have been written during a lockdown when things were quiet and predictable. I realise how right Gustave Flaubert was when he said, 'Be regular and orderly in your life, so that you may be violent and original in your work.'

After I reread it, I felt I had been touched by the spirit of Anne Desclos (who wrote *The Story of O* because her husband challenged her that a woman couldn't write a book like *The 120 Days of Sodom*), and in dialogue with books I have read and loved, in particular *By Night in Chile* (Roberto Bolaño), *Season of Migration to the North* (Tayeb Salih), *Their Eyes Were Watching God* (Zora Neale Hurston), *The Lover* (Marguerite Duras), *Story of the Eye* (Georges Bataille), *Woman at Point Zero* (Nawal El Saadaw), *I Remember* (Joe Brainard), *Hour of the Star* (Clarice Lispector), and *A Girl is a Half-formed Thing* (Eimear McBride).

*

'ኩሉ ይሓልፍ ፍቅሪ ትቐጽል – *kullu yihalif, fiqri yiterif* – *everything passes, love remains*', is a well-known Eritrean proverb.

Samuel Beckett's *Not I* inspired the sections of the *EYES*.

Zora Neale Hurston's *Their Eyes Were Watching God* inspired the line: 'I looked at the pool of water in the distance, and as if I saw an ocean with ships on the mud-puddle, my imagination sailed into the bay of BB.'

The poems quoted from in the book are:

> 'I Like My Body When It Is With Your' by E.E. Cummings
> 'Sister Outsider' by Audre Lorde
> 'Instantes' attributed to Jorge Luis Borges
> 'Dream Variations' by Langston Hughes
> 'Aedh Wishes for the Cloths of Heaven' by W.B. Yeats.
> 'The Lady's Dressing Room' by Jonathan Swift
> 'L'Idole, Sonnet du Trou du Cul' by Arthur Rimbaud
> 'If You Forget Me' by Pablo Neruda (translated by Donald D. Walsh)

Other novelists and poets who make an appearance are:

> Virginia Woolf
> James Baldwin
> T.S. Eliot
> Sappho
> Anna Akhmatova
> Dorothy Parker
> Paul Verlaine

Song lyrics quoted are from:

> 'Something Got Me Started' by Simply Red
> 'Freak Me' by Silk
> 'Close To You' by Maxi Priest
> 'Always Look on the Bright Side of Life' by Monty Python

The Seers by Sulaiman Addonia
Published by Prototype in 2024

The right of Sulaiman Addonia to be identified as author of this work has been asserted in accordance with Section 77 of the UK Copyright, Designs and Patents Act 1988.

Copyright © Sulaiman Addonia 2024
All rights reserved

No part of this publication may be reproduced, stored in a retrieval system, or transmitted, in any form or by any means, electronic, mechanical, photocopying, recording or otherwise, without the prior permission of the publishers. A CIP record for this book is available from the British Library.

Design by Matthew Stuart & Andrew Walsh-Lister
(Traven T. Croves)
Typeset in Marist by Seb McLauchlan
Printed in the UK by TJ Books

Standard edition: ISBN 978-1-913513-51-1
Special edition: ISBN 978-1-913513-61-0

(type 2 – prose)
www.prototypepublishing.co.uk
@prototypepubs

prototype publishing
71 oriel road
london e9 5sg
uk